'Hig... ...attempt to
evol... ... way to tell
a person's story'   John Boyne, *Irish Times*

'Written with imagination, great assurance and a painterly eye, it
builds up a fine portrait of the city'   *Scotsman*

'A wonderful book, unique and surprising, alive to the energy and
mystery of New York'   Joe Dunthorne, author of *Submarine*

'A short book with a big bold sweep. It pulses with the life of the
great city and rattles along with its energy'   *Daily Mail*

'Vivid, full of deadpan humour and very, very unusual'
                      Emma Healey, author of *Elizabeth is Missing*

'New York City as a creative catalyst is an enticing subject matter
and one that receives a delightfully unexpected treatment in
Bradbury's elegant debut'   *GQ*

'By interleaving a series of parallel New York narratives spanning
120 years, she makes that great metropolis seem intimate, its
inhabitants connected across the decades by shared desires'
                                                  Daily Telegraph

'A kaleidoscopic dreamscape of New York seen through the eyes
of some of its most celebrated inhabitants . . . immersive and
compelling'   Olivia Laing, *New Statesman*

'In a narrative about art, creativity and vision, she shows the flair
of an artist . . . Megan Bradbury's idiosyncrasy and chutzpah are
a fitting epitaph to a city that, as F. Scott Fitzgerald put it, has
the 'wild promise of all the mystery and beauty in the world'
                                                            Herald

'Fascinating, almost a work of philosophy . . . Bradbury makes
connections between people and places, and across time, that are
edifying and moving'   *Herald Scotland*

Everyone is Watching

Megan Bradbury was born in the United States and grew up in Britain. She has an MA in Creative Writing from the University of East Anglia. In 2012 she was awarded the Charles Pick Fellowship at UEA and in 2013 she won an Escalator Literature Award and a Grant for the Arts to help fund the completion of *Everyone is Watching*, which is her first novel.

MEGAN BRADBURY

Everyone is Watching

PICADOR

First published 2016 by Picador

First published in paperback 2017 by Picador
an imprint of Pan Macmillan
20 New Wharf Road, London N1 9RR
Associated companies throughout the world
www.panmacmillan.com

ISBN 978-1-5098-0976-9

Another version of Chapter 17 first appeared in Issue 214 of *Ambit* magazine (2013).

1 3 5 7 9 8 6 4 2

A CIP catalogue record for this book is available from the British Library.

Printed and bound by CPI Group (UK) Ltd, Croydon, CR0 4YY

Visit **www.picador.com** to read more about all our books
and to buy them. You will also find features, author interviews and
news of any author events, and you can sign up for e-newsletters
so that you're always first to hear about our new releases.

For Ben

*While this novel was inspired by a real city,
and by the lives and work of real people, it should be
treated as a work of fiction. Where it is based directly
on existing works, these are acknowledged
at the end of the book.*

'Longing on a large scale is what makes history.'

Don DeLillo, *Underworld*

1

Robert Mapplethorpe rips out a page from the magazine and cuts around the guy's torso, leg and dick. He sticks these parts onto paper. He lies in a dark room in Brooklyn. It is 1967. He hears other people moving around the house. He has a feeling that time is passing without him. The feeling is acute and in the pit of his stomach. It is the vibration of the subway that he can feel.

When he walks across the Brooklyn Bridge he feels on top of the world. The subway is filthy and alive. The clatter of the trains is music. The graffiti inside the carriages is art. The ascent from the subway to the sidewalk is an ascent into heaven. In the busy downtown streets he never feels alone.

One night in his dark room in Brooklyn Robert is woken from a dream. Bright light frames a figure standing in the doorway.

I'm looking for someone, she says. Do you know where he is?

She turns her face away from Robert, into the light.

He is awake. His eyes are open. He cannot speak.

Robert sees this girl again in the store where she works. He originally came for just one beautiful thing, the Persian necklace in the window, but now there is also this girl.

The girl is reluctant to let the necklace go. She wants it for herself.

I will only let you buy this if you promise to give it to me, she says.

This girl will claim in later years that they were always destined to meet – it will be one of the things they talk about – how God did it, or the devil – bringing together two sides of the same person.

As Robert walks home to Brooklyn he fingers the necklace in his pocket. He feels its weight. He remembers the rosary beads he used as a child. How many Hail Marys for this, he wonders.

Robert sees the girl again in Tompkins Square Park. The black sky is filled with stars. They don't seem so far away tonight. The drawings he will make later will be related to space and the afterlife, two things that are magic because they can never be touched.

Suddenly this girl is upon him. He believes her to be a repetition or affirmation of his thoughts. She is talking very fast. He will agree to anything she says – just look at her.

They zig-zag through the city blocks. She is faster than him. She is pulling him on. He is flying, not weighted any more. Her name is Patti. He says his name is Bob.

Oh no. Can I call you Robert? she says.

Robert comes from Floral Park in Queens. Floral Park is a still life study where everything has been neatly arranged. Everyone's front door is painted the same colour. Everyone's lawn is cut the same length. Outside each house hangs a star-spangled banner that flips over in the breeze and freezes in winter. Outside there is a swept pathway and an unspoilt lawn.

Eight-year-old Robert Mapplethorpe is sitting on the living-room rug in Floral Park threading beads on a string for his mother. He is making one of his first necklaces. The TV is turned down very low. Robert peers through the fog of cigarette smoke, engrossed in his activity. The rug – soft and warm under him – and his mother close, the flicker of the television in the corner of his eye, this bead then this bead, arranging as he goes. He never makes a mistake. Each bead is placed in the order of his desire: this bead and then this bead then this bead.

Robert's father takes the one hour and twenty minute commute into the city every morning, and he doesn't complain.

Here he is sitting in the subway car, reading the morning paper. He stands to let a young woman sit, folding his newspaper into quarters, hanging onto the leather strap, swaying with the movement of the train, the brake and acceleration, reading his newspaper in segmented intervals. He will have read the whole commentary section by the time he gets into New York.

In his spare time Harry Mapplethorpe collects tropical fish and stamps. He is also a keen photographer. He develops the photographic prints himself. It is not the finished product that interests him but more the process of the photograph's creation.

Robert attends Catholic classes. The devil makes his stomach flip. He is the character that makes things happen. Sin is something to ask forgiveness for but Robert doesn't believe in God. Robert believes in magic. Robert likes the rituals of the church. He likes the rosary beads and the crucifixes. He likes the way objects are arranged on the altar. He likes to carry the candles and wafers for mass. The incense fumes make him dizzy. The priest tells him that God is always watching. Robert likes the idea of someone watching him.

Robert is sitting in a closet in his Floral Park home amongst the sheets and blankets, flicking through the pages of a nudist magazine. He looks at the bodies on display, women playing volleyball, their heavy figures lunging forward, the sculpted men beside them, muscles taut and flexed. Robert begins to masturbate. He can smell washing detergent and warm towels. He looks at one image then another, one body then another, body to body to body.

Robert Mapplethorpe will learn to say, 'Floral Park was a good place to come from in that it was a good place to leave.' This is what he will say when he is famous. He will learn to make the distinction between the place where he comes from and the place he lives later.

———

Sixteen-year-old Robert heads straight to 42nd Street. He dodges the bums, the pimps, the businessmen, weaves in and out of traffic held up at lights. He tries to duck into a movie house but he doesn't have any money – the clerk waves him away, letting others through. He feels sick. He figures this is the Catholic Church trying to take a bite out of him so he tells Christ to go fuck himself and runs down the street. He needs to see something. He stops outside a magazine store he knows well. When two men walk in, he ducks in behind them. He creeps along the magazine rack, scanning the covers as he goes. The magazines are sealed in cellophane and the cocks are covered over with tape. He stares at the magazines. He realizes that *this* moment is the one he wants to fix down – *this* moment, *this* feeling in his stomach. He wants to cut out the photographs and make his own art from the guys and their dicks. He grabs what he can and he runs.

But the storeowner and a man standing at the counter have been watching him the whole time. They knew all along what he would do because, had there been stores like this when they were young, they would have done the same goddamn thing.

Stop him, Joe!

The man blocks Robert's way.

What you got there, kid? Some weekend reading? What do you want me to do with him?

He's got a sweet face; leave him be. You don't mean any harm, do you, boy? What's wrong with you, kid? Can't you speak?

Robert kicks the man in the nuts and runs.

There's nothing like New York for a kid who wants to get lost in the crowd.

In 1963 Robert attends Pratt Institute and joins the Pershing Rifles fraternity. He wears a dark military uniform and stands in line. He is stripped, blindfolded, and made to perform a drill. The end of a rifle is pushed into his anus. A brick is tied to his penis and he is ordered to throw the brick across the room. These activities do not penetrate his exterior. He does whatever he is told. He wants to be pushed to an outer limit and thereby be changed. He is developing a hard shell. He is transforming. He wants to belong. He wants to be someone.

In the summer vacation of 1964, when Robert is seventeen, he operates the games of chance in the Belgian Pavilion at the World's Fair in Queens. On his lunch break he eats waffles from the waffle stand. Sugar grains stick to his fingers. Today is a clear day. Families, kids in baby carriages, holding balloons and balloons tied to the handles of baby carriages; they pause at the church entrance, looking up at the high tower. There is music playing at the carousel. The skirts and jackets of the children are a blur as it spins. The children are laughing.

Robert sucks the sugar from his fingers and crosses the square. He looks along the open concourse towards where he knows Manhattan is, but all he sees is an impenetrable mass, twin sets, grubby T-shirts, candy-coloured summer jackets, thickened, roller-set hair, kids on roller skates, yanked back by the scruff of their necks by their mothers, the suited men, hats – they spill through the entrance and swarm the walkways, hot dogs in their hands; they are coming straight for him, heading towards the monorail. They have their money ready.

The high lines of the monorail and cable cars score the sky. He sees high-rise pavilions and viewing platforms from where people are watching the fair. He sees the swinging legs of the public. They arch and lean to see below.

He pushes his way through the mass and walks back towards the Belgian arch. He must get to Manhattan where he can be himself. He hears babies crying and sees kids running through the arch towards the fountain and the central lakes lined with international flags. Tourists spill in from Manhattan with ice creams, the sticky grip of babies' hands. He is not one of them.

Robert cuts around the picture of a weightlifting man and fixes a red transparent circle over his crotch. He is making collages out of the things that he finds. These subjects are the things he wants to look at most. But the teachers at Pratt don't like Robert's work. They don't understand what he is doing. They ask him to explain himself, but he cannot explain. He leaves Pratt because it's dangerous to know too much about something. There are too many teachers in this place. He is not a student anyway, never was, never will be; he is an artist.

—

7

You don't understand who I am! I am an artist! I am somebody! But Robert's father won't look him in the eye. His father won't look at him at all. He doesn't like the way Robert dresses. He doesn't like the way Robert talks. Get out of here, his father says. Robert packs his bags. Robert takes the subway to Manhattan. The pace of the train is the pace of his pulse. This is what happens when you are the centre, the focal point of everything. There is nothing to see – a black hole – you turn to look but find nothing there. Here is Robert Mapplethorpe moving from the outside in, heading right into the centre of Manhattan.

2

Edmund White steps through the automatic doors of the terminal and joins the line of people waiting for a cab. It is 2013. Suitcases and holdall bags punctuate the sidewalk. The people before him crane their necks to watch for cabs that will come very soon.

Edmund closes his eyes.

He sees the parking lot and the city, his past and his future, bright blue sky. New York. Ashen, acrid, remorseless. Edmund sucks his dry tongue to the roof of his mouth. This is unpleasant. Hasn't slept. It's not easy, this turning back.

In the cab, as he goes, billboards merge at high speed. Here are the cemeteries of Queens, the rush of the dead. I am old, Edmund thinks, shielding himself from the sun. He rolls down the window – exhaust fumes, dirt. The driver taps on the plastic shield, points to a sign – *Don't Roll Down The Window; This Cab Is Air Conditioned.*

They come at the city over the Queensborough Bridge through an arcade of steel supports that criss-cross the view, the East Side vista, the gap-toothed grin of Manhattan, fomidable graph, blocks high and long, stuttering behind erect supports. They plunge into Midtown.

Here, spring is passing. A sunny haze lingers over Columbus Circle and the entrance to Central Park. Here is the willowy lightness of London plane trees. People sit by the fountain, watching a man play a saxophone that shimmers in the sun – golden. They lounge, limbs outstretched, easy.

Edmund stands outside an apartment block on West 30th Street. He turns to see his reflection in the glass foyer door. He is wearing a crumpled cream suit and a blue tie. The tie is crooked. His cheeks are flushed; he looks as though he has been dragged here against his will. He taps the glass door with his finger. He has a headache. His headache may be because of the sun. He lived in New York many years ago and he knows a New York summer gets inside of you. His publisher's assistant, when she comes, will show him this apartment. He waits on the sunny side of the street. He cleaned his shoes back in Paris. Here, the leather shines. Perhaps it is the pressing-down of time he feels and not the sun.

He used to spend his summers on Fire Island. The parks in Manhattan have always been contrived while the dunes and beaches of Fire Island are wild and natural. Back then, he wanted to strip off his clothes, walk freely in the sunshine, and bathe in the ocean. He was relaxed and calm, a young man with a future. His whole life seemed as clear as the water, as inviting as the warm sand. Fire Island was his island. A solitary land mass filled and then emptied of people. Men shielded their gazes with hot brown hands.

Long Island is growing large from an accumulation of sand caused by moving tides. This new land changes the context of what is already there. He doesn't know what to make of a place that keeps expanding.

Every year American beach grass has to be planted by hand to keep the dunes from washing away. He doesn't know what to make of a place that, if left to itself, would simply disappear.

This is always what it is, thinks Edmund. Despite memories of free abandon, it was really rules that held everyone in place. He knew it then and he knows it now, that, besides sex, what lurked behind those sand dunes was time. We've all had our experiences, an interviewer once said, though I can't help thinking Edmund White is still right in the middle of his.

Edmund White?

He turns around to see a woman with a clipboard and an outstretched hand. I'm sorry to keep you waiting, she says. Shall we go inside?

They enter the cold-blasted, air-conditioned foyer.

I like the name White, she says. It's like the beginning of something fresh, like clean sheets.

She presses for floor number five.

The reflective surface of the elevator door shows a distorted Edmund White. The assistant beside him is reading his vital statistics on a piece of paper, secured to the clipboard by a shiny metal lever: Edmund White; one-bedroom apartment with easy access to subway and mainline transportation; Monday; lease tbc.

His apartment in Paris had doors that opened out onto

a balcony overlooking the roof of a church. Chilly breezes rustled papers. The sound of gentle rain. Conversations. French flowing in like the breeze. Edges, rough and unfinished. History, one he didn't know. Language, something he didn't understand. Breathing, shaky and uncertain. The bulk of a lover, warm and alive. Time stretched out, delicious and permanent.

This L-shaped apartment is only temporary. Its position on the block is determined by its hard, straight edges, its squareness, the angle of the floorboards as he stands here, the hard edge of the window with its black frame and sill. Nothing can come in or go out. The windows are sealed shut and the air-conditioning unit is whirring. The towels in the bathroom hang neatly in a line. His stomach is as tight as a nut.

Soon, he will pick a nice place in Chelsea or the Upper West Side. It will be a place that suggests a future. It will contain many things to do, fix up, put right. He will go out and buy new furniture, art, paintings, bookcases and books. He will have his old belongings delivered there. He will get right back down to work. He will set out all of his notebooks on the table. He will read every page. He will organize his life into chapters. He will examine a map of the city. He will write about what things were like in the past. He will remember the city's dirty streets. He will remember himself. He will remember when it all began for him, in the 1960s, when he arrived in a city that was on the verge of collapse, the city and him. He will align this theme of the end of the city with the notion that, for him, things were just beginning, like someone had switched on a light for Edmund and he could finally see the world.

The assistant switches on the kitchen light and opens the bedroom door. The temporary bed is pushed up against the wall. There are grey marks on the surface of the mattress. Edmund possesses no sheets. He will have to go out and buy sheets. He will have to go out and buy a good many things – clothing and kitchen utensils. They will all be new and unused. He will unseal the window to let the air in.

I have papers for you, the assistant says, laying her briefcase on the couch.

She opens the briefcase and takes out the papers. There is a run in the back of her left stocking. Her stocking is a veil. I cannot touch you, Edmund thinks. He watches how she handles the paper. Pages flick. She is not in any hurry. She has no other place to go. She likes to be here with Edmund White. Edmund White is a famous author. Edmund White has written many books. She will ask if his signature is the same as the one he uses for the inscriptions in his books and he will say he cannot remember. He will say that he is not a machine, that he cannot simply sign book after book without consequences. He will say that he is not the same as his author photograph, which was taken many years before. He is not that man. That is another Edmund White. You think that man is me but that Edmund White, *that* Edmund White, is a stranger, a man from the past. That Edmund White is just a man in a photograph.

3

Robert Moses is looking out of the window of a train at the towns and villages of Long Island. It is 1922. He is catching glimpses of the ocean, the glittering sun reflected across it, boats sailing there. As they come out of a town, he sees woodland in the distance that covers many acres. He doesn't know what this land is used for. Then it's gone.

Moses loves the town of Babylon on Long Island where he is renting a bungalow with his wife. He can stroll through the quiet streets and down onto the beach. He can swim alone in the ocean. He is forceful yet elegant when he swims. He cuts through the water without a splash – he glides. He likes the ocean best when it is rough. He likes to work against a strong force. To watch him from above would be to watch a machine, the direct line of movement through the water caused by his body, those thick, broad shoulders, the wide, defined back.

Robert Moses is busy working hard for the governor but there are many other things he wants to do. Most New Yorkers don't get the chance to swim in the ocean. Children play baseball in streets that are congested with traffic. They swim in the East River, which is polluted with waste. Families live in overpopulated tenement slums with no access to gardens or public parks. Summers in Manhattan are unforgiving. People can die without relief. Those with automobiles drive to Long Island. But what looks like an hour's drive on paper can, in reality, become four hours along such inadequate roads. Everyone is trying to get somewhere else but there is nowhere to go and no way to get there. People sit in traffic for hours at a time. They slowly pass the estates of the richest families in America, the Morgans and the Vanderbilts. They pass the columns and gated driveways, the turrets of castles, the lush mani-cured lawns of the rich.

As Moses walks home from Babylon station, he thinks about the patch of woodland he sees every day from the train. No land should be left unused.

Robert Moses pays a visit to the Babylon Town Hall and asks to see a map of the island.

That woodland out by the coastline, he says to the clerk, what's it used for?

It's the old Brooklyn water supply, the clerk says. A place to store water in case of a shortage. Never been used, as far as I know.

Robert Moses obtains the use of a car and a driver. He is driven through Long Island along Merrick Road. At the end of the road he gets out of the car and climbs over the fence into the wood. He picks his way through the undergrowth, through the bracken and the wild grass, through bramble thickets. This is not just any wood but three thousand five hundred acres of forest. He finds four reservoir ponds with lilies growing there, and pickerel and trout swimming. He finds a reservoir bigger than that in Central Park. He can see it all in an instant, recreational parkland with tennis courts, baseball diamonds, and a golf course, picnic tables, hiking trails, lakes used for swimming, and enough space left over to build a road directed towards the ocean and a brand new public beach.

Moses reads about the legends of the Great South Bay, about the shipwrecks and the fishermen there. He asks local oystermen about the island: which parts are unexplored? How can he get to them?

Moses buys himself a small boat. His wife calls it the *Bob*. He goes out in the boat alone and scours the Long Island shore. He is looking for hidden coves, fjords, dunes and forests.

There is a sandbar called Jones Beach just off the southern coast of Long Island that's completely inaccessible except by boat. Moses lands his boat and drags it ashore. He sits on the deserted beach, which stretches as far as he can see, snow-white sand reaching east and west.

Moses explores Jones Beach, walks up and down it. He sits and thinks. He walks through the undergrowth and wades in the ocean. He swims. Floating in the water, he looks back at the sandbar.

———

Again, Moses throws his lunch into the *Bob* and heads out. It's smooth sailing, just the glassy water beneath him and his own shadow cast across the boat's hull. Not another boat to be seen on the ocean. Not a cloud in the sky. He is heading east to Fire Island, the next barrier beach. He cuts the engine and pulls the boat onto the sand. He shields his eyes from the sun. He walks through the sand dunes, the beach grass, the wild marshes. These things don't appear on any of the maps he has seen. The place is clean and wild. Pure. Not polluted and overcrowded like Coney Island, no bawdy barkers or scandalous sideshows. No freaks. It is a natural place. This is the perfect environment, a clean slate. And it is growing. He finds himself in the middle of many acres of beach when, according to his map, he should be standing in the ocean. The tide has produced new land by doing what it does naturally. This is value produced by the passage of time, he thinks.

Moses struggles against the powerhouses of City Hall, the institutions, the go-getters, the populists and idealists, the moneymen, the landowners, the engineers, the governor and the mayor. They all tell him no. They tell him there's no money for this. They tell him nobody wants the roads and the bridges, and nobody cares about public beaches. The Governor Al Smith isn't one for sports and recreation. He doesn't like to watch baseball. He would never run. But this is the man Moses must convince.

Al Smith was born in the Lower East Side in 1873. He learnt to swim in the East River by diving off ramshackle piers into the polluted water with his friends. The trash floating in the water was just part of the scenery. Smith's whole world existed in the Lower East Side, for this was where the whole world lived, the greatest concentration of different nationalities in America. The streets were his playground, his recreation yard, the dark alleyways the running lanes, burst drains the waterholes, loose sidewalk stones the obstacle course. He witnessed the completion of Brooklyn Bridge from his tenement window. His family were Irish and Italian. He understood what it was like to be an outsider and to take advantage of opportunities when they came. He wasn't educated like the other politicians. He didn't understand the politicians when they spoke. He did not know the process of drafting a bill. He took the bills home and he read them all. He read everything he could to help him understand. He was not privileged but people liked him. He had a certain way with people. He could look a fellow in the eye. He told a man straight what he knew. He knew everyone in the neighbourhood. He knew what life was like for them. He lived, not in wealthy uptown housing like the other politicians but downtown.

So why take a shine to Robert Moses? This Yale-educated, professional, literary young man? Did he see the makings of a good human being in that sparkle in his eye? Was it Moses' ideals that he approved of? In the beginning, Moses had many.

Moses makes Al Smith get out of the car and he points to where the parkway will go. He explains the layout of the bridge approach and the crossing to the sandbar off the coast, which will be Jones Beach.

Moses says, This is where the central parkway will come over and the entrance to the east bathhouse will be here, and on either side of the causeway will be parking lots, and just there will be the refreshment house with a boardwalk running along the outer edge, and the beach beyond that. Lifeguards will be stationed at regular intervals, and we will put the locker rooms beside the first-aid booth, and there will be services inside those locker rooms: lavatories, showers, lockers and diaper-changing rooms. This is where the theatre will go, a curving outer wall and stone benches, and there will be bathrooms and dressing rooms back stage. There will be swimming pools and diving pools, sun loungers, chairs and tables, and a restaurant beside that. Further along will be the games area, shuffleboard, table and paddle tennis, roller-skating rinks and a pitch-and-putt course. And here, an area for additional shade. Beach grass will be planted by hand to keep the dunes in place. Can you see it, Governor?

My God, says Smith.

In 1924 Al Smith appoints Robert Moses the head of the Long Island State Park Commission. Moses takes his security and the chauffeured car and he walks through the back gardens of the properties on Long Island, flashing his new City Hall credentials. He notes down the dimensions of the land. He measures with tape and takes photographs.

He instructs his men to do the same. When he looks at the stately mansions, he is looking right through them. He does not see the protests from the owners at all. He is seeing what this land could be without these houses, without these men standing in his way.

Al Smith takes Moses by the arm and they stroll through the Lower East Side. They walk down Orchard Street, along Delancey, up the Bowery, pass over to Mott Street. They walk through the crowds of people huddled over goods for sale in the street market stalls. Smith stops to shake a few people by the hand.

Al! they say. How's Katie? Let me shake your hand.

Smith says to Moses, This is how a city is run. You have to be prepared to shake hands with ordinary people.

Moses visits one Long Island farm on a number of occasions. At first, he is the most charming man the family has ever met, suit jacket slung casually over his shoulder as his broad figure strolls across the open fields. He stops to take in a deep breath of air. The family are waiting for this important man to speak. It is as if he has seen a little piece of heaven in what they are doing here. Hell, they think he is going to give them money to see the whole place preserved as it is. Inside the house, Moses helps the mother to make the coffee and talks about his childhood in Connecticut, how wonderful it was to live in all that open space. He asks the mother about her own children: Are they healthy? Do they enjoy living in the country? He explains that for

Manhattan's children it's not so easy – the lack of space, the dirt, disease. If the children were taken out of Manhattan and shown this farm they just wouldn't believe it.

But it won't stay that way for long, says Moses. The developers will get here sooner or later and they'll tear this land up to build new houses. Soon the whole of New York State will be a sight to see, nothing but houses. The thing to do is to make parts of this region accessible to everyone. Allow those who live in the city to visit here once in a while. You should see the faces of these children. If you did, it would break your heart. All I need to do to improve their lives is to build one straight road from Brooklyn to Long Island. This is where I'm building my beach. How's the farm doing? Moses asks, not to the father but to the mother. Her hesitation says it all. I'll give you a good deal on this land. The road won't be anywhere near the house. You'll have enough money to buy more land elsewhere.

We don't want more land, the father says. We don't want your money.

I'll let you think it over, Moses says.

We're not selling, says the father.

Moses picks up his jacket and his hat. He thanks the mother for the coffee and wishes them all goodbye.

Next time, Moses brings with him an army of suited men. He walks into the kitchen and drops the new plans onto the table. He says that the money he is offering is now half the original amount. And the road, which before ran up over the brow of the hill, now runs beside the house.

The father says, You can't do this – I'll get a lawyer, I'll—

Moses laughs.

Within six months they lose the farm.

Merrick Road needs to be widened and turned into a parkway, and two other parkways must be built to connect Long Island to the sandbar. He will need to build a bridge across the water to the island, and he will need to raise the sandbar to make it high enough to build upon. He does not seek the approval from the owners of the estates on Long Island. Moses comes onto their land and measures up. They see him from their bedroom windows and call security. Moses returns with an armed guard and approval from the governor. The landowners take Moses to court, and for a while it looks like Moses might lose his precious beach. He is criticized for not going through the proper channels, for not negotiating with the other side. He has just waded in with fists flying.

Being reasonable doesn't get things done, he says.

Moses waits for the season to turn hot when everyone is in the mood for beaches. Then he addresses the court, describing the conditions for ordinary people on sweltering New York days with no space for recreation or refreshment while the richest families in America use Long Island for their private playground. Now the papers have a story. *Savior Moses. Hero Moses.* He is one for the people. *Where's Our Beach?! Dying for the sake of a little fresh air!*

Moses has realized that if you are for beaches then you are for the public. It's so hot that everyone is for beaches. The whole city has gone beach mad.

What the courts don't know is that Moses has already started to build his beach. He has bulldozed the woodland and laid the foundations for access roads. He has measured out the perimeter dimensions and brought in all the materials. Now what court in this country is going to order the reversal of hundreds of thousands of dollars' worth of work?

He says, Once you sink that first stake, they'll never make you pull it up.

4

Richard Maurice Bucke is standing on a railway platform on a crisp, clear morning in 1891. He is waiting for Walt Whitman. What he sees is the hustle and bustle of people waving through the polluted air with hands and pocket books. Other passengers climb aboard the train for the beginning of their journey but this moment marks the beginning of the end of Bucke's, for he and Walt will part company when they reach New York City.

In his hand Bucke is holding a notebook in which he will write another biography of Walt. Thinking of the original biography now, it seems inadequately slim and out of date. He could write five or six more volumes about his friend.

Bucke first encountered *Leaves of Grass* when he heard it being read at a party. Afterwards he felt a series of impressions held together like beads on a string. It was no longer the real world he knew but the world left behind in the wake of poetic revelation. Bucke rested in a valley between exact reality and poetic truth, for suddenly he possessed the words but not the man. Bucke wanted the man. He found him eventually in his home in Camden. He spoke with Walt at length about his poetry. Bucke has been trying to describe his friend ever since, but the more Bucke writes the more he finds he cannot prove him. He cannot set him on the page, pin him down, pin him to the ground. Walt is magnificent. Bucke remembers riding home from the party and experiencing a feeling of light and fire. He felt the world fall down. This feeling has remained. It is not easy to live with the sudden knowledge of possibility, to feel it in the blood, hot and terrible.

Bucke moves to the centre of the platform. Beyond the railway the horizon is a shimmering line. Porters throw bags on and off the train. What Bucke is seeing are the definite actions of strangers about to form new lives, perhaps he is also. He is ready. He is waiting. But Walt is always late.

Walt is watching a porter leaning against a stack of trunks. It is as if the trunks are an extension of his body; they are as tall and as solid as he is. This man is lost in a dream. He hears no noise, no hiss of steam, no voices. These trunks will eventually be separated and restacked within the carriage and this man will be left upon the platform. Walt will sit within the train and the train itself will depart. Perhaps he will see this man from inside the train, waiting on the platform as the train moves on.

His friend Bucke is writing another biography. It will be another souvenir of Walt's life. Walt wants this great book to be written. It will help Walt remember the places he's been.

He was born on Long Island. He often stood on the shores there and felt the great spray of ocean spatter his face. He walked across the sand and sat down in the beach grass. This was where he read his books. He explored the coves and beaches. He found rare shells and milkstones there. He kept them all as souvenirs of the place he loved most.

The first ships landed at Long Island. Sailors pinned their shaky steps onto its golden shores and headed west to Brooklyn. Brooklyn was lush and hilly then with wild open space and undulating vistas. What the men saw was possibility. They realized they could use the land. They looked at Manhattan and they said, No one lives there. It is too hard to live there. It is difficult to get to. Nothing will ever grow there. Brooklyn was where the crops were grown. Brooklyn was where the seeds were sown. Brooklyn was soft and penetrable. Grass grew. Men built houses, churches, beaches, ports and piers. This is where Walt is from, from Long Island and from Brooklyn. Walt is going home to that hilly, fertile place.

5

Patti and Robert drag a mattress back to their apartment in Brooklyn and scrub it with a scrubbing brush and bicarbonate of soda. Robert picks out black sheets. He jokes that Patti is his sacrifice. They set up altars and paint the walls.

They adopt a routine called 'One Day–Two Day'. If one of them is down the other has to be up. This is the only way they can survive. It is a great responsibility. The presence of one makes the other feel whole.

One day Robert goes to a gallery and Patti stays home. The next day Patti goes to a gallery and Robert stays home. They describe to one another what they saw. Patti is better at this than Robert. Often, Robert spends so long getting dressed up that by the time he arrives at the gallery the building has closed.

The best artworks Patti makes are the gifts she gives to Robert. She makes Robert an advent calendar. Behind every door is a picture of her.

Patti once stole an encyclopaedia from the local store in her hometown. She stuffed it under her shirt, but the fucking thing was huge.

Show us what you have there, miss.
She pulled the book out from beneath her clothes.
This all you got?
What else is there? she said.

Patti tells Robert many stories. He doesn't know if they're real or not.

Patti gets a job in a bookstore so Robert can work. Robert works all day and waits for Patti to come home. He lays out all of his pieces so that she can see what he has done.

Patti has a faster metabolism than Robert. He can go for days without eating but she is close to collapse by lunch-time if she has had nothing to eat. Robert loves chocolate milk, but it is expensive. She wants to point to her skinny body and say, You have done this, Robert, you and those fucking milkshakes.

Robert heads to 42nd Street for a hot dog – gone in two mouthfuls. He talks to the guys on the street. No money for dinner but he likes chocolate milk. Gone are the days he used to know. Here is something else. Street life.

Robert and Patti move into a room at the Allerton Hotel on Eighth Avenue in Manhattan in 1969. Robert is shivering with fever on a mattress. Patti is mopping his brow. She sits beside him all night as he sleeps. The morning comes slow and grey. She hears the hotel manager outside the door. He hammers on the door but she doesn't answer. She holds her hand over Robert's mouth. She opens the window and looks out. She sits Robert up and dresses him. She hoists him up against her shoulder. She pushes him onto the fire escape. She looks back to see if she can carry anything else. There are too many things but not enough time. She pins a few paintings under her arm and follows Robert. On the sidewalk she hails a cab. Take us to the Chelsea, she says.

Robert is slumped in the reception of the Chelsea Hotel. Patti is talking to the man behind the desk. She flattens her pictures out and points to what they are: art, the future, what they will one day be.

Robert is sitting in his room in the Chelsea. He is threading beads and charms onto leather bands. He is making one of the first necklaces that he will try to sell. Laid out upon the floor is all of his and Patti's work. Art. It lies all around him, in this room and in every other room of the Chelsea. It seems the whole world is made up of art.

Robert adorns himself in necklaces. They are made of feathers, skulls and plastic beads. He calls them Fetish Necklaces. They remind him of the rosary. People are praying all the time in the Chelsea. They talk to themselves as they walk down the corridors. They sleep at night with their bedroom doors open. Voices echo through the hallways. The skylight over the staircase lets the sunlight and night light in. Robert clutches the beads and prays for success.

———

Robert hustles on the street with a friend to make some money. It's just a way to help pay the rent. He asks his friend how he knows he's not gay. Because however cute the guy is, his friend says, I always ask for money. What the men ask Robert to do is kids' stuff, anyway. And he needs the opportunity to express himself. The street is the perfect place for this. These experiences are helping him to define who he is.

The artist Sandy Daley gives Robert a camera. Sandy says he should be taking his own photographs. Robert thinks this will make his work more authentic. This way he can position his subjects however he wants.

The photography curator at the Metropolitan Museum of Art, John McKendry, likes Robert's art very much. He thinks it shows a strong classical lineage. Robert's male nudes remind John of the work of Thomas Eakins, the nineteenth-century artist who painted and photographed young men, showing them as beautiful objects to be admired. John McKendry befriends Robert Mapplethorpe and Patti Smith. He wants to find ways to help them both. He gives Robert a camera. If there is ever a problem they can always count on him.

Robert will say later that he was young and naive at the Chelsea. He will say that he was standing on the edge of an art scene. He is standing on the edge but he is also crammed into the middle, crammed into the small room that he shares with Patti and crammed into the city. An artist is influenced by the people around him. He must learn from others how to become a success. You have to be part of a scene to do that.

There is a steakhouse on 18th Street where all the artists go called Max's Kansas City. Robert and Patti are hanging outside the joint.

We just have to walk in with our heads held high, says Patti.

She takes Robert by the hand and pulls him in. The din is extraordinary. The booths are full, jukebox music, shots of whisky lined along the bar, men and women speaking loudly together, thick tobacco smoke, the smell of char-grilled meat hanging in the air. Everybody here is very young. There are groupie girls with fur coats and fake eyelashes, drugged up to the ceiling, they fawn and lean, asleep. They float. Everybody is looking at everybody.

A bottle of beer will buy you a seat at the bar. This is what Patti and Robert do. They sit at the bar and drink the beer. They try to look casual. They watch the artists in the booths. Patti knows that this will be them one day, and so does Robert.

That's already us, he says.

Patti and Robert have outgrown the Chelsea. They need more space for themselves and their art. They move out of the Chelsea and into an apartment down the street. There, they set to work.

—

Robert props up the mattress against the wall and in comes the model, Robert's lover, David Croland. He poses against the mattress, arm outstretched, wearing one of Robert's necklaces – a leather band and a shark tooth.

Here is the mattress on its own, grey, dirty, thin lines running down and pinned at points.

Here is Robert Mapplethorpe looking up into the camera. His face is blurred. He is looking for something.

Here are Polaroids of Patti Smith. She is standing behind a screen door, lying on a sofa, lying on a messy floor with headphones on.

Robert still thinks about God, the devil and his family. They come into his head when he is low. When he is high, he rises above all feeling; he becomes connected with the wider universe. This is to do with the people he is watching and the people who are watching him. Something is created in the space of the gaze. It's not something he can explain but he feels it physically.

Art collectors visit Robert's apartment. They look at Robert's slides and installations. The problem they have is with the subject matter. Enormous cocks are not the kind of thing people want to hang in their dining rooms, but they like Robert's cool, eclectic style, the negatives he hangs from pegs on the wall, a pair of unworn patent shoes under the closet, a single tie folded on a shelf.

The viewfinder of Robert's camera has become a self-determining edge. Robert places his eye against it and looks at the world. Here is the world as he has never seen it. Click. Here are all the people he knows and loves. Click. Here he is. Click. Here are the different parts of his body. Click. Click. Click. Here are the subjects as he has arranged them. Click. Here is a collection of classical male nudes. Click. Here are the men standing on plinths like marble statues. Click. Here he is pinching the shutter balloon.

Robert makes his male subjects mimic Greek statues positioned on plinths, framed, himself included in a sequence of consecutive moments –
  the robe,
  him wearing the robe,
  taking the robe off,
  holding his cock,
  robe hanging on a hanger,
  naked figure fallen forward from a plinth,
  man talking on a telephone with his legs crossed and his trousers down, his heavy penis slung over to one side,
  Polaroid of a telephone shot from the height of the table.
  Robert's new lover, Sam Wagstaff, in the bath,
  washing his hair,
  shaving his chin,
  looking at Robert.

Later, a headshot of Robert wearing a black leather jacket with the collar turned up, smoking a cigarette, the smoke curling up past his Teddy boy hair, background black, he is looking at you.

(You wish he was)

A body shot of Robert posing with a knife.

Their friend John McKendry has become very ill. Patti and Robert visit him in the hospital. Robert says he doesn't want to go. Robert says it will be depressing. Patti pulls him on.

At the hospital Robert looks about the room, anywhere but at John, who is sitting upright in a hospital chair, wearing a hospital gown but no shoes or socks. John stares at Robert. The nurse explains that John has been running the ward as if it was the Metropolitan Museum of Art. He has been writing his name on the walls. He doesn't have very long to live: Alcohol is destroying his liver. He is going slowly mad because of the toxins. Robert can't stand the hospital. Robert takes John's photograph.

Robert Mapplethorpe says photography is the perfect medium for the 1970s because everything is happening so fast. Now that Robert is in possession of a camera, Robert will not steal pictures from pornographic magazines any more. He will take pictures from his own life and use them in his work instead. That way, he is in control. That way, he can make people do what he wants.

Robert goes to Max's alone. He goes in the late hours, breezing in through the door like the regular he has become. He is often the centre of attention, not because he is a great artist yet but because he is so fucking sexy, his tight leather pants and fucked-up jewellery, the long curly hair and cold green eyes.

He strolls right up to the bar and orders a drink. He walks up to the people standing there. I'm an artist, he says. Who are you?

6

In the past Edmund regularly saw psychiatrists. They explained to him that his homosexuality was just a symptom of wider issues: his tendencies existed because his mother was overbearing; he was simply looking for attention; it was because he didn't get on with his father.

Edmund did what he was told for periods of time. He avoided other boys and stood up to his mother. He lowered the tone of his voice and pretended to like sports. He abstained from everything the doctors said, except for the sex part, which he treated as a reward for all of his efforts. Then he moved to New York and found another doctor. Dr Silverstein told Edmund to just live his life. Dr Silverstein was concerned only with time.

He said: It's a mistake to think of life as series of chapters. Time doesn't stop and start with every life event. Thinking of it like that is just your way of shirking responsibility. You think that if all moments are isolated then it doesn't matter what you do. But everything is connected, Edmund. You are the person you are because of your history, and the things you will do in the future will be informed by your past. Tell me, Edmund, is this what you're writing about?

———

Edmund is trying to remember New York. He reads his notes:

Late 1970s – the state of the city is fully realized. New York's reputation is changing. Tourists = investment. The New York Department for Economic Development commission an agency to transform the city's brand. The agency keeps coming back to the word 'love'. They turn 'love' into a slogan. 'I Love'. 'I Love New York'. New York becomes a symbol – NY. They turn 'love' into a symbol, a heart, I♥NY.

7

Robert Moses is standing on Manhattan's western shore in 1934. The ground has deteriorated and is crumbling into the Hudson. He is standing in the lapping river water there. The oily slick is coming up over the toes of his shoes. He kicks away the refuse and walks to steadier ground. The railway line behind him is sinking. Carriages are rusting in the sidings. The landfill used to expand the island is breaking apart. Yet just a few hundred yards away is a modern metropolis, a centre for business, manufacturing and art. This wasteland has no place in a city that contains the Empire State Building, that emblem of engineering achievement. Standing here you could forget you were in New York. The Depression has hit the city hard. It's not recreation people are thinking of now but jobs. The only way to improve people's lives is to improve the city. Moses is the man who knows what needs to be done. He's not like the city planner who draws pretty pictures to just keep on file; he is a builder – he creates.

Planners have already tried to improve conditions downtown by raising the railway tracks from street level onto an elevated line. Before, when the trains ran along the ground, cowboys were employed to ride in front to warn road users of their approach. Despite the holler and alarm, the accidents continued. So the trains have been lifted into the air.

The public can now look out from the upper floors of tenements and factories and see trains passing by their windows. But this solution is already outdated. It is the automobile and not the train that is the transport of the future. It is a highway and not a railway that needs to be built.

Moses will build a road here. Drivers will use this road to bypass the city entirely, no need to stop at every junction or wait in line along narrow, sunless streets. No more breathing in the noxious fumes coming from the building vents and sewers, no more watching workers shuffling along the sidewalks. No, the driver along this road will see the sun reflecting off water and a public park where people play sports. This driver will become the master of his day, cruising down a clear road.

Moses buries the railway underground and he builds a parkway over the top. He builds new sports facilities: tennis courts, baseball diamonds, basketball courts, running tracks and playgrounds. He builds handball courts. He plants trees and flower borders. His road allows traffic to bypass the city. It means the public can get to where they are going quicker, go out further, beyond Harlem, and right through the Bronx.

8

Let's go back to the construction of Brooklyn Bridge, says Walt. I was there when the first support was laid in 1870, and I was there when the bridge was completed in 1883. As I walked across the bridge I thought of my humble printing press, what it did – I thought, It is the same, for both the bridge and the press allow ideas to move freely. I thought, There is now nothing to stop people from walking across the water to tell someone else what they know. I crossed the bridge and looked down at the river from a great height. I looked at the river that rushed beneath me. I realized we were no longer reliant on the passage of ships. I thought about the many trips I had made to Manhattan by ferry, and how that would now be changed. The bridge has changed everything, Bucke. We can now walk across the East River. We have never been able to do that before. It makes me think that anything is possible. But Bucke, we mustn't be frightened.

Walt rode the Fulton Ferry when he was young. As he sailed from Brooklyn, the ferry leapt in the wakes of cargo and passenger ships. It was a great sport, first thing in the morning, sailing to Manhattan. The captain, who was standing beside Walt, laughed at the bucking of the waves, and so did Walt. Walt felt his body lunge out beyond the borders of its skin, beyond the ferry, beyond the city. He

watched the dock fast approaching, the harbour men waiting on the pier, their heavy shoulders tired from work,
bodies sloping forward. They were watching the boat come
in. Walt laughed. No one heard him above the slapping of
the waves.

Walt walked away from the river, up South Street,
through the boatyards and the fish stalls. He stopped to
converse with the fishermen there. About him was the
briny extraction of commerce, fish eyes and fish scales.
He smelt the smokeries and the tanneries on the dock. The
ground was flooded with water and fish guts. He picked his
way through the debris. All life was here, the fishermen and
the boat builders, black-eyed men. He loved them all.

He saw a flower seller, a coal merchant, an omnibus
driver, a beer-hall keeper, street-sweeper, a banker, politi-
cian, prostitute, factory worker, young children playing
in the street, a courting couple, a horse trader, a rigger, a
sailor, a soldier, a nurse, a milliner.

When he reached the Battery, he leant against the wall
at Castle Clinton and looked across the bay to Brooklyn.
He saw the boatyards, the long-arm reachers lifting cargo
from the ships, holding their loads steady. It is only from
another vantage point that one understands what one is
looking at, and he was looking at it, looking back at Brooklyn from the southern tip of Manhattan, with the rest of the
city tucked safely behind him. Something was bound to
happen in the future. It was like he had already written it.
It was like it was already built.

Walt remembers when the great Lafayette visited the

city when Walt was just a boy of five or six. That afternoon, the road was filled with people. The public of Brooklyn waved colourful flags and shouted from the sidewalks and from the upstairs windows of buildings. Lafayette stopped his carriage and helped lift children to safety. He picked up little Walter and kissed his cheek. He went on to lay the corner stone of the Brooklyn Apprentices' Library. Every time Walt passed that building he thought of that great man. That building is now torn down. Lafayette's visit is lodged permanently in Walt's mind but not in the physical fabric of the city. Places grow up from the people who live there. Every footstep, however slight, marks the ground. As a house builder, printer and poet, Walt is concerned with the way things are created. Here he is walking through his imagination, held safely by the present environment – the carriage of a train – but he is thinking about New York.

Bucke watches Walt begin to doze. He is tired. He has let his hat fall to the floor. How quickly these states of consciousness change, thinks Bucke.

He remembers the time when Walt visited him in his asylum in Ontario and became lost amongst its wards. Bucke looked for Walt in the wards and in the gardens, and when he couldn't find him he returned to his office. He pulled a few books from the shelves. They were not his books but his father's. He had brought them from the house after his father had died. He liked to keep them here in his office. He used to spend days alone in his father's library, permitted to read anything he liked. He read literature, science and mathematics. Over time he saw how each sub-ject was connected to the next. Bucke is a psychiatrist. He earns a living by performing scientific tasks yet he gains his pleasure from art and from poetry. Walt says there is no difference between art and science. Everything in art is exact and correct and everything in science is beautiful and profound. This was what Bucke was thinking of when he heard a commotion out on the lawn. He discarded the book and moved to the window. Someone, it seemed, had found Walt. He was sitting on the lawn surrounded by patients. The patients were listening intently to his speech. How easy he is with all people, thought Bucke. He will talk to a guard, a professor, the mentally disturbed. They are all the same to him.

9

John McKendry forces his way through executive crowds, down the dark ravine of Wall Street, then Pearl Street. He crosses the road and marches through Battery Park towards the water's edge. He carries in his jacket pocket a twelve-thousand-dollar ruby necklace and a ten-thousand-dollar set of diamond earrings. He had walked into Tiffany's with the intention of buying a sapphire. It was because of a dream he'd had – a clear blue lake that he could not penetrate. He did not want to jump because the water was so still and reflective – he thought it was glass. In the dream, he peered for so long that very soon the water became the sky, and then he realized he was upside down. In that moment of realization, he fell. He peers into the water now but sees no reflection in the wild, choppy bay.

In his archive John McKendry lays out the photographs on the table that he will show to Robert Mapplethorpe. Robert must understand how his work relates to the art of other photographers. It is essential that John choose the right photographs to show his protégé. These photographs show New York City throughout the twentieth century. Here is New York during the Great Depression as seen in the work of Berenice Abbott. The city is not modern yet; here is a horse and cart in the street and a skyscraper in the distance. Here are Lewis Hine's pictures of workers balanced on scaffolding high above the city as they build the Empire State Building. Here are the photographs of Jacob Riis: children sleeping on fire escapes, men sleeping on flophouse floors, families sewing garments in dirty tenements. And here are McKendry's favourite photographs: the posed male nudes of Thomas Eakins bathing in a water hole. They are clean and untouchable. They are perfect.

In the Metropolitan Museum of Art, John stares at the suits of armour standing to attention. There are no bodies here – no men and no horses. Armoured gloves joust at nothing – they have no hands. John raises his own hand to his body as if he too contains these gaps. He discovers again the contents of his jacket pocket. He is clutching jewels he cannot afford to keep.

John McKendry dreams about Robert Mapplethorpe. Even in the daytime, even during dinner. When his wife Maxime says, *How was your day*, his mind is already filled with Robert. They're making a mess of the new wing, he says. But the mess is inside his head. The rubies and the diamonds feel heavy in his pocket. They are no longer amusing. If he gets them out now, Maxime and her son will barely raise an eyebrow. This kind of behaviour is what they've come to expect of him. Tomorrow he will take the jewels back to the store.

———

John McKendry's favourite opera is *The Makropoulos Case*. In it, the main character takes the elixir of life and lives for ever. John cries throughout the intermission. At the end, John remains in his seat even when the opera has finished and the audience has left. If he moved, he would become involved in a sequence. If he moved, he would become tangled in chronology. The ushers eventually tell him to leave. He stares at the empty stage. The characters have gone. He doesn't want to die. It makes no sense.

John McKendry himself is small and feminine and his body has no shape. It is grey and fleshy. There is nothing to it but it always seems so heavy. His head isn't right. He is out of proportion. There is a problem with the way he carries himself. His limbs are pushed out into the wrong places. His poses are unnatural. He is gangly, small. He is unexciting. Nothing ever happens to him.

John McKendry once fell in love with the moon. It seemed obvious; its face was very beautiful. He saw the face reflected in the surface of a lake. He thought – I love that moon and perhaps that moon loves me. It was partly because of the distance between them. John McKendry saw the moon reflected in the lake as he positioned himself for the dive but also in the mirror, which he had broken. He lay upon the broken glass, bleeding as easily as he wept. The tears formed a lake, or was that blood? The whole thing was hilarious. He thought – How easily I fall in love.

His flesh was torn by broken glass. He thought – I have been penetrated – the glass that reflects the moon now enters my body and we are lovers. I make love to the moon. It is over too soon. He never returns my calls.

John McKendry just had to be with the moon, he had to go out there and he had to reach for it, so he opened up the balcony doors and he climbed out onto the exterior wall. He did not fall – it was not that – but back inside the hotel room he saw the reflection of the moon in the mirror, and he ran to it, and the mirror smashed, and he lay there on the glass, bleeding, and that was it. He nearly bled to death. When he got home he recreated the scene for Maxime and it was hilarious, for he could not walk. He staged the whole thing, even the part where he was lying on the floor bleeding, and he could not get up, not because he was bleeding this time but because he was stuck there, owing to old injuries. Maxime walked out. She could not see the funny side. She did not come back until that evening when she returned to find him in exactly the same place as she had left him, only this time in the dark, despite the moon being full.

They move John into hospital. The staff are non-committal about preservation. They are here one minute and gone the next. They do not follow orders. They run things their own way. Researchers come with their overcoats and clipboards – sometimes they bring tourists with them to observe – they get in his way. They sit down and ask him questions that have nothing to do with Robert Mapplethorpe. One time they stick needles into his arm. They have moved him into a room with windows. Here, he can see the city. At night he can see the moon. He is over it. There is too much work to be done. These people do not take art seriously. The pictures on the wall are low rent, tacky. Something has happened to all the other pictures. There are spaces on the wall where the pictures should be. There are too many electrical sockets. It is good that the researchers wear rubber gloves. They will not ruin the photographs. He must get rid of these people. He must fire them. He fires them all. His rubber gloves have disappeared. Without the gloves, he gets ink on his hands. Now they are angry with him for marking the walls. But what is he supposed to do if they don't give him any gloves? They tell him to sit down but he is already sitting – do they want him to lie down? They say someone is here to see him. It won't be the person he wants but the vision that comes in through the door is the vision of what he's always wanted. It is too cruel, this final view. He cannot look at Robert Mapplethorpe. He looks up into the air instead. There is a blinding light. He thinks of lightning and the white surface of the moon, what it must be like to have the mind completely clear and finally wanting nothing.

In Robert Mapplethorpe's photograph, John McKendry's face glistens in the light of the flash. Freckles cover his skin, ears, eyelids. He looks up. On the wall behind him there are two sockets. The first, complete with plug, is positioned in the top left-hand corner of the picture. The second socket is unoccupied. Next to the sockets is a blank rectangular panel, painted white. The photograph has been cropped in such a way as to suggest a link between John McKendry's face and the panel. John McKendry does not seem aware of the camera. He looks as though he has let go of something and is watching it float away into the air.

JONES BEACH, 1929

No ballgames. No nudity. Bathers must shower before entering the pool. No bobby pins. No jewellery. No outside food or liquor.

Gee, they know what they want, the boy says.

Regulations, says his friend.

The boys move through the parking lot and under the expressway. They enter Jones Beach by way of the east swimming pool. They carry towels over their shoulders and an illicit supply of Scotch in a beaker wrapped in a lilo, rolled in a duffel bag. It is the weekend. This is what summer will mean from now on, weekends at the beach.

The first boy loves the newness of the signs and the crisp-neat uniforms of the pool attendees. His friend loves the brass-band music coming from the pavilion and the ice-cream sellers in candy-striped boaters.

They stand beside the swimming pool. The first boy has never seen a diving board before except for the pier in the East River where he so often launched himself in summers as a kid before the rot took it under. Then, you would swim in fear of your life for the river was cold, dark and deep. Here, the water is clear.

The girls come giggling down the path. They are dressed in matching bathing suits. They clutch their handbags in the crooks of their elbows. Their sunhats are bigger than Liberty's crown.

What are you boys waiting for? says one.

Nothing special, says the second boy. The girls drop their act. Have they come all this way to be insulted?

We're watching the divers, the first boy says. Wanna jump with me?

The girls' humour is quickly restored. Easy with this boy. Forever the clown. Safe with him. Looks good in the sun. Nice and tan. Can see his future. It's all mapped out. Could go far with him. He'll take you out of the city. He'll find you a new place to live. He says he wants to be a newspaper reporter. He could be your ticket out of here.

They settle on a bench to watch the divers. A woman is standing way up on the high board. She's a real beauty. Bright red swimsuit and matching red cap. Her body is as tight as the heat of the day. She is a dream, needs rescuing – what the first boy would give to – yessir – this is the right place to be, watching from below, not a thing he can do in the world except watch. You can't fight nature. He feels the first girl's upper arm pressing against his. The woman on the board stretches herself into a pointed rocket – hard, sleek, silhouette against the sun.

She caught your eye? says the second boy. Not a question. Caught his also. Have you ever seen anything like it? he says.

He has never seen anything like it.

They flock to her, the boys, the men. Watching from below. Moving closer.

The clean concession stands and squeaky-clean attendants gleam in the sun. Smiles beam across the water. Everyone's eyes are stinging from the chlorine. This place is clean all over. The woman on the board could have been hired for the part, she is so beautiful. She is brand new, without a story. She makes the first boy feel like a child. He feels fresh. He never wants to take another drink in his life, or do anything unclean.

The woman curls her toes over the edge of the board, dizzy at this height, and the ocean in the distance, and the men crowding round the pool, jostling for position.

Jump! cries one. Then they all cry – jump! Jump! Get that sweet ass in the pool. The lifeguard blows his whistle and points to the sign – No ogling.

Sweet ass!

The lifeguard marches over and hustles the man away.

Jump, will you?!

She is already falling.

10

Edmund unpacks the rest of his books, those about France and the travel books and the biographies he wrote about Arthur Rimbaud, Jean Genet and Marcel Proust. Next he unpacks his novels. Then come the works of journalism and memoir. Here is the entire range of Edmund White: the Edmund White who is him, the Edmund White who is based on him, and the Edmund White who resembles him only.

He looks down at his hands. His fingers are long and slender. His knuckles are red. His palms are fleshy. They have held many other hands. The cuffs of his shirt pinch his wrists. His right wrist is strong from decades of writing. His arms have encircled many bodies. His chest is soft and tender. It contains his beating heart. His stomach has consumed the world. His hips are the parentheses for what lies in between. His penis is cold and independent. He has described it in the pages of these books.

He picks up another book he's brought back from Paris, a book about the photographer Alvin Baltrop. The black-and-white photographs contained within it depict New York scenes from the 1970s. They show the Hudson River Piers when they were dilapidated and deteriorating. The roofs are loose and the floorboards are broken, yet life exists here nonetheless. In the photographs naked men lean against sun-bleached walls. They share cigarettes, conversation, oral and anal sex. They are kissing. They are sleeping. They are hanging out.

Edmund remembers that the vast interiors of the piers could alter one's perception of reality. In the same way, these photographs, presented as they are from the vantage point of present time, also mean something new.

These photographs show human interaction as blades of grass growing through the hard earth. The subject depicted is love.

Edmund picks up his own novel, *Hotel de Dream*, whose main subject is the writer Stephen Crane. The book describes Crane's last days and a novel that he is rumoured to have written about the life of a young male prostitute he once met in the Bowery. Crane's book, if it exists, has never been found. In the absence of the real thing, Edmund wrote it himself.

He discovered that in order to write about the American Civil War in *The Red Badge of Courage*, Crane studied photographs taken during that period. He looked at the work of Mathew Brady and Alexander Gardner, the black-and-white photographs of desolate battlegrounds, gaping-mouthed corpses, shadowy figures in distant fields, fallen men lined in neat rows in the grass, portraits of distinguished soldiers and commanders, the wise, chiselled faces of Abraham Lincoln and Walt Whitman.

Edmund tried to be as thorough with his own research. He read many books about New York at the turn of the twentieth century and he looked at many photographs. He walked in the footsteps of Stephen Crane, imagining another time. He walked through the Lower East Side and examined the low-rise tenements, imagined the slums and the dark, narrow alleyways. This was where gangs of boys lurked in the shadows, where filthy laundry hung strung up between the buildings in a latticework of depressing garments. He imagined the cries of babies going hungry and bedraggled prostitutes half-dead in the street. Edmund put himself in another time and in another reality. By writing about real subjects in the form of a story, he created a book that was both fact and fiction.

He called the prostitute in the story the Painted Boy. This boy still seems very real to Edmund.

He stands on a New York sidewalk. He is young and naive. He has no family or connections in Manhattan. He learns to survive by selling himself. He hustles on the street and in local theatres. He doesn't fully understand his power over people. He takes money from the men who love him the most.

Looking at the novel now, Edmund wonders what it is really about. Could it be that he, Edmund White, is the Painted Boy? Or perhaps he is the writer Stephen Crane. Crane was a journalist and a novelist. Crane wrote fictionally about real life. These things are also true of Edmund White. The main theme of Edmund's work is love. Edmund has carried love around with him his whole life. Love has accumulated like time. Edmund carries love with him still. He has brought it back from Paris, the city of love. He runs his fingers along the spine of *Hotel de Dream*. His signature is written upon the title page. Here is his photograph on the jacket. When Edmund looks at the photograph he is staring back at himself. Edmund has called this book a fantasia on real themes provided by history. Here Edmund stands in the flesh in the twenty-first century.

11

Next, Robert Moses tackles Central Park. He brings in heavy machinery and a large workforce. He brings in lights and generators. Workers work in shifts, twenty-four hours a day until the grass has been sown and the flowers are blooming. He installs more playgrounds with play equipment for children and benches where their mothers can sit and talk. He puts in bathroom facilities and diaper-changing rooms and special ramps for baby carriages. He cleans out the shanty town that surrounds the menagerie. He pulls down the menagerie and builds a zoo. He cleans up the reservoir. He carves out pathways that stretch in all directions. He seeds ball fields. He provides spaces where the public can move. He refurbishes the castle. He plants trees to line the mall and he cleans up the fountains, scrubs lichen and moss off the benches. He allows only the best concession stands to sell ice creams and hot dogs and pretzels there. New gates are fixed, erected and painted. The sidewalks surrounding the park are tidied and cleaned and replaced where broken. A permanent workforce is established to maintain the park. The workers water the grass. *Keep off the Grass* signs are erected. The Ramble is tidied. The shrubberies and trees are cut back. The paths are swept clean. The bridge over the boating lake is painted brilliant white.

12

The sun has fallen behind the mountains. When the porter comes in to turn up the lights, Bucke turns them down. Walt is sleeping. He is lying across the seats, his hat on his chest, his overcoat pulled over his heavy frame, which the seat does not comfortably hold. He could be mistaken for a travelling man. Bucke knows he has visited many places.

Walt is dreaming about the great World's Fair that came to New York in 1853. It is a glittering palace made of glass, and through its walls he can see the people of the city. He stands on the edge of Reservoir Square to admire it. The tower beside it is three hundred and fifteen feet high. From the summit of that tower Manhattan, Queens, New Jersey and Brooklyn can be seen.

Walt searches for the American exhibit. He thinks of the poetry he has been writing and how America is contained within that too. Here is the country shown through the objects created by its own citizens. They have brought their livelihoods to New York to be displayed. Everything laid out in front of him was made in America. Spread out before him on the tables are surgical instruments, chronometers, clocks, telescopes, philosophical instruments and products resulting from their use – a telescope, a portable illuminator, an electromagnetic telegraph battery, barometers,

thermometers and glass hydrometers, instruments dismantled and presented, daguerreotypes: portraits of men,
women and children, framed and displayed behind glass.

On other tables he sees examples of different types of
cotton in various forms – handkerchiefs, tablecloths, cotton
lines for drift nets, wool, silk, velvet, furs and leather –
materials made directly from nature. There is a working
model of a steamboat. He looks at an exhibit of stationery
and bookbinding, embossed show cards, India-rubber ink
erasers, specimens of writing inks, prayer books, Bibles,
writing paper; he knows these items well. New mechanisms
for carpenters, machinists, manufacturers and the product
of their labours: church bells, steamboat bells, umbrella
and parasol stands, tea sets, pottery, tools for dentists, gold
pens, glass, twisted tobacco pipes, and a pianoforte.

He passes an exhibition of rocks and minerals taken
from across America. Stones cleaved in two glitter and
shine. The public pick them up to feel their weight. He
moves past them all.

He finds what he is looking for, *Christ and His Apostles*,
the white plaster figure of Christ with his head solemnly
bowed, the twelve apostles his audience. Walt looks from
statue to statue. He is very small and they are very large. He
wonders what these statues could possibly mean in a world
that is capable of producing all the other items on display.
Are these statues so large because we wouldn't know the
subjects otherwise? If Christ exists then he is our size and
walks amongst us. He mustn't be set aside to admire.

Walt joins a gathering crowd. People are watching a

demonstration by a man on a platform that has been hoisted into the air. The man is holding up a pair of shears and he cuts the rope that secures the platform on which he is standing. The crowd gasps but the platform holds firm. The crowd applauds and cheers.

What will happen in the future now that elevators exist? Bodies pushed into a box and raised high. It will change the landscape of the city. The city will grow vertically. When people are close enough to touch the heavens will they feel closer to God?

Walt dreams of the prison ships moored off the Brooklyn shore during the Revolutionary War. Prisoners are kept below deck. The only light to penetrate shines through the iron grate above their heads. Men rely on the whims of unsympathetic guards. Men sit in the dark and await their deaths. This stinking hole has become their whole world. The prisoners are dying of disease or are killed for insurrection. Their bodies wash up on the Brooklyn shore. When the weather is rough, the sand blows away, revealing a pile of bones buried beneath. The people of Brooklyn are outraged when they find them. They demand a proper burial site. They demand a memorial. God will not find these men if they remain buried here. There is a great parade in the men's honour. The men are buried deep in sanctified ground. Life grows from them. Blades of grass.

I have been dreaming, Walt says.

Bucke covers him again with his overcoat and strokes

his aged cheek; it is dry and warm. He traces the lines in Walt's skin and thinks of the layers of age visible in rock. Walt closes his eyes. Bucke turns down the lamp. He imagines Walt standing on the Long Island shore when he was young. Walt's breath is like the breaking ocean tide. All things are the same, his breath, the movement of the train as it passes across America, the tide of an ocean a thousand miles away. This is what Walt meant by his description of Brooklyn Bridge. It is no great revelation to see how things are connected. Bucke is able to visualize the bridge because Walt has described it, and now he is joined to Walt through this image. It is a connection that will survive all time and distance. Bucke closes his eyes and thinks of the bridge. The breeze coming in through the open train window is now the wind coming off the East River as he stands halfway to Manhattan, halfway to Brooklyn.

DAY TRIP, 1920

Before Jones Beach, before Robert Moses, a father packs his family into a car and sets off.

It's bumper to bumper all the way. An hour in and they've not even made their way out of Brooklyn. The father looks over at the car beside them and sees kids crying in the back seat and Grandma overheating. His wife is silent. The kids are starting to complain that they're hungry. He tells them to eat whatever they want. He'll get more food later, he says, when they arrive at the beach.

They crawl through Long Island towns. At last he sees the entrance to a beach, but there is nowhere to park along the bank. A uniformed guard waves the cars on.

The father calls out the window, What's the problem?

The beach is full. Please move along.

As they drive further east he looks at the ocean. Miles out to sea and nothing is there. The father can imagine the cool water and the gentle breaking waves against his body. Lying there, floating in the water, looking up at the blue sky above him, diving deep below the surface, moving his body to its extreme, his family watching from the beach.

Another forty minutes and they've made it to a fishing village with signs to another beach, but as he swings the car into the entrance a guard steps into the road and holds up a hand.

There's no room. Please move along.

The road has become a dusty trail. The father has to roll up the windows to stop the dust getting in. But it's too hot to have the windows closed so he rolls them back down.

At the remote tip of Long Island, the father scans the banks until he sees the entrance to a beach where the gate is open and the land beyond is clear.

At last, he says.

But as he turns the car into the entrance a man emerges from the bank and commands him to stop.

This is private land, he says. Please turn your car around. There are public beaches to the west, sir.

They're all full.

This is not a public beach. Please move along.

But this beach is empty!

Please turn your vehicle around.

He does what he is told.

He drives back the way they came, through the towns.

His wife wakes up and looks at the ocean that is now on the other side of the car but she does not ask him to explain. The kids stare out the window at the fields and the woodland.

Don't worry, kids. I know where we can go, he says.

———

The father pulls the car over before the Brooklyn Bridge approach. He orders his family to get out. They cross Fulton Street and walk towards the East River where tankers and sailboats are passing on the water and traffic rumbles over the bridge. They walk towards the palisades. He climbs over the barrier and onto the sand. He kicks the dirty cans to the side of the beach. He takes off his shoes and socks. He walks towards the grimy water. He looks back at his family. They are watching him in silence. He steps into the river. The water is cold. The oil-slicked surface of the water encircles his ankles. His family doesn't follow him in. They don't move from their position on the wall.

13

Robert Mapplethorpe tells the man to look left, look right. The man won't smile unless Robert tells him to smile. Robert catches a view of New York through the window. Whether or not it can be seen in the photograph, this is where his subject has come from, from the streets of New York.

There was once a man named Robert Opel who lived in San Francisco. Imagine it: the Golden Gate Bridge, sunshine, hills, streetcars moving up and down the roads, easy afternoons in the Californian sun, the Castro, store doors sprung open, a cool ocean breeze, the occasional vehicle ambling. Imagine being this far away from New York. Everyone says this man is Robert Mapplethorpe's doppelgänger – a controversial artist prone to naked stunts and famous for riling up polite society. He has a female partner who writes poetry – another Patti Smith, people say. This Robert dies very young. He is murdered, shot down in his own gallery. They say it was a robbery, but, you know, what kind of gallery keeps cash on the premises? Robert Mapplethorpe would never be caught up in anything like that. He has a knack for slipping out of places before there is trouble.

—

At an art exhibition in Midtown, Robert looks at mannequins displaying cancerous tumours. The tumours in some
cases are very large. His own shadow is cast across the floor
in between the models, in between disease. The beauty of
New York is that when you turn around there is always
something worse to see.

He walks out onto 42nd Street and everything is the
same, tumours all around him, people, disease, and the
opposite: physical perfection, the human body, perfect
fomations, the casual stroll of a figure, the running of a
body across the street, skin as smooth as marble, faces like
glass, the demarcation of muscle in an upper arm, a neck,
a frown, the extended line of a pointed hand and finger, an
arm reaching up. The body is an architectural structure
with an external form holding everything in.

14

A few weeks ago Edmund received an email from a fan named T asking if the two of them could meet. T is an actor in his thirties. *You should meet me, I'm cute*, the email said. Edmund quickly responded.

Now Edmund is waiting for a reply from T. He is tired of pretending he doesn't care. He wonders if T is one of the men he is passing in the street. It could be him, or him, or him, he thinks.

The traffic along Eighth Avenue is a gushing river. Edmund White feels the thunder and rattle of trucks, the stifling sun, suppressed beneath awnings under which he is passing, pausing, tired out by the merciless crowd. He turns down 34th Street, looks into a hole cut into the road, an intricate web of pipelines and cables bathed in artificial orange light. He cannot see where the cables reach; the hole is too deep. Workmen pass buckets up and deposit their contents into a dumpster. The dumpster seems too close to the edge of the jagged hole.

Edmund turns north up Fashion Avenue, pausing to look into a bead-store window. He looks at the buttons, ribbons and bows, mannequins, and fabrics trimmed with lace. He crosses the avenue. A *70% Off Closing Down* sale sign has faded yellow. The window shows a row of ugly mannequins displaying prices, divas from the seventies, dressed in sequined evening gowns and crooked wigs. They stare out at Edmund. He walks into the shade of 40th Street, past the parking garages and garbage depots, crosses Broadway. The traffic is one continuous boom. Something inside of him is expanding. The people who pass him create small gusts of air. The traffic moves, caught ahead, moving on. Heat, miserable, folded in layers, he is connected, spiked through, pinned down, trailing threads, losing time – it spills – building up, how long, hours? Years? Decades? He is incredibly hungry. The snack carts wilt in the shade. Dirty yellow sun umbrellas, rain umbrellas, advertising signs. He looks ahead at the space of Sixth Avenue. There is the entrance to Bryant Park. A truck accelerates, revealing an oasis of green.

The fountain gushes. Busy people walk clutching coffee cups, confident, wealthy, healthy, lie stretched on fold-out chairs, sit lined up in the sun, legs in the sun, feet up on a wall – work break, lunch break – busy – business dates, lunch dates, salad bowls scraped with plastic forks, cans of soda emptied and crushed. Legs pushed up against the roped-off lawn. Don't step on it, now. Do not step one foot upon the grass. There are the stop-start honks of traffic on the avenue. Buses hush to a pause. Babies scream in off-road strollers. Edmund struggles through them all.

Here is the outdoor Reading Room. The shelves are lined with books. Sparrows are bathing in the dirt.

Edmund sits in his regulation fold-out chair. He can see the Empire State Building behind a black tower that is decorated with gold. Kindergarten kids are passing him. They clutch rope circles that are tied onto a long rope line. One boy is proudly singing his alphabet.

Edmund remembers when Bryant Park used to be empty of people except for the homeless and lonely men. Now the public are sitting on picnic chairs, reading newspapers, peering into lunch bags, balancing laptops on their knees, closing their eyes against the sun.

The long branches of Bryant Park trees hang suspended over the path where he is sitting but he does not feel protected. He looks up at the Empire State Building. He can see the windows and the window blinds clearly. Grey clouds move behind the building. They do not penetrate exterior walls. This is what it feels like to have it not go in, to find out that one's body and soul are too hard. I used to be as tall as the Empire State Building. Once upon a time I stood higher than the rest. You could see every eyelash, every speck of colour in my eyes. I was not afraid to be seen in detail.

Edmund used to segment the city according to different types of lovers. There were the eye-openers of Greenwich Village, the seedy males of the Meatpacking District, the gaudy show-offs of Broadway.

When he wrote *Hotel de Dream* he imagined Stephen Crane's Painted Boy. He imagined what it was like to want the thing you cannot have, to see it standing in the street, to speak with it, touch it, but to never have it for yourself.

The lawn of Bryant Park is lush and green. Sparrows peck at the neatly shorn blades. Edmund watches two women talking at its edge. They have made their way down from the bar to smoke cigarettes. One slips her stockinged foot out of her high-heeled shoe and places it delicately onto the restricted grass.

15

1936 is Moses' swimming-pool year. He opens the renovated Hamilton Fish Pool and Bathhouse in Manhattan on June 24th. This pool is large enough to accommodate over two thousand swimmers and holds 485,000 gallons of water. There is a diving pool and benches with planted trees for shade and a wading pool, locker rooms and playing fields for sports. On June 27th the Thomas Jefferson Pool and Bathhouse is opened in Harlem providing relief from hot summers for the people in the surrounding tenements. On July 2nd the Astoria Pool and Play Center opens in Queens, positioned in front of the Triborough and Hellgate Bridges with views of the Manhattan skyline. It is big enough to accommodate 3,000 people and is lit by underwater flood-lights in the evening. On July 7th the Joseph H. Lyons Pool is opened on Staten Island to a crowd of 7,500 people. The Highbridge Pool and Bathhouse in Manhattan on July 14th, the Sunset Pool in Brooklyn on July 20th, the Crotona Pool in the Bronx on July 24th, the McCarren Pool in Brooklyn on July 31st, the Betsy Head Pool in Brooklyn on August 7th, the Jackie Robinson Pool and Recreation Center on August 8th, the Sol Goldman Pool in Brooklyn on August 17th.

Moses likes to swim. He swims whenever he gets the chance. He will swim morning, noon or night. He is for-midable in the water.

16

Walt's dress shirt is hanging over the waistband of his trousers. Bucke's own clothes are pressed and tidy. This is the difference between the two of them. It is something Bucke cannot ignore. Bucke wants to look smart for Walt. Walt has not changed his clothes in several days.

Don't you think we should send word ahead to the engineer? Bucke asks.

The figures in the car through which they are passing are relaxing before dinner, reading books, sitting quietly. There is a mother bouncing a baby on her knee.

Walt laughs. He is determined to see how everything works.

When they reach the engine carriage they see a man standing before the furnace. He is blackened with dirt but his eyes are bright.

Walt shakes him vigorously by the hand, dirtying his own hand.

How much will she take? Walt says.

Whatever we give her, she'll use.

May I try?

Walt throws logs into the furnace. What fun he is having.

Look at me, Bucke!

—

Bucke is watching. Bucke sees everything very clearly. Time is moving too swiftly. Times are changing. Train travel is becoming popular. High towers are being built. People can now climb to the top of a building and see the boundaries of a city. They can see where things begin and end. These boundaries don't appear to concern Walt. Here he is playing with the engine of a train as a child would. Walt is not the age he is physically. He doesn't notice any contradiction in the world. Walt describes the city as if it was a natural place. To him, the city is as natural as the woodland, as calming as the ocean. He describes Trinity Church and Castle Clinton as if they had grown right out of the earth. At other times, he says that the wonder of the whole universe can be found in the form and structure of a single leaf.

Walt wants all the things he cannot have. He says that when he is in one environment he is sure to be longing for another. For the hustle of Fulton Street, he says, or his beloved Broadway when he is looking at Camden's streams and fields. The city holds treasure for Walt. But Bucke is an expert on the mind. This is where real treasure lies; it can be found in human consciousness. By developing consciousness we can learn to see from above. Walt sees from above. Even when he is asleep and disconnected from his surroundings Walt sees everything, while Bucke can only see boundaries and borders, lines preventing one thing from connecting with another.

—

Walt is writing a letter in the dining car. He is hunched over the paper, consumed by his writing. Bucke is working on his manuscript. It occurs to Bucke that he and Walt are not sitting in the same place. They are both together on this train but they are separated – one is in his letters and poetry, the other in his biography.

Walt is writing to Peter Doyle. He is explaining that it would be far easier for Peter to visit him in Camden when he goes there later in the year rather than Walt travelling to Washington. He is feeling very tired. He thinks he has eaten something that doesn't suit him. He must be more careful with his diet. His appetite has not changed with age.

He crosses this out and begins another letter.

He writes that he is feeling better than he has felt in a long while, yet there is so much work to do back home that it would be best if Peter were to visit him rather than Walt travelling to Washington. When could he come?

Walt folds the letter then crushes it into a ball and stuffs it into his jacket pocket. He stands up. He waves his napkin as a goodbye to Bucke.

Bucke watches him go.

In their compartment, Walt is describing the assassination of Abraham Lincoln as if he had witnessed the event himself.

Did you really see this, Walt? asks Bucke.

In a way, we all have seen it. Either we are sitting low down in the centre of the stalls or we are perched high upon the balcony. It depends who is telling the story. The position of our imagining shows others who we think we are. I used to see our president in the camp. One morning he crossed through the medical unit and stopped to talk to the soldiers there. He shook the hand of every man he met as if he was a friend.

Bucke remembers the first occasion when he heard *Leaves of Grass* being read at a party. He listened to *Leaves of Grass*, then he met the man. The feeling was the same.

Dream of Life
(1996–2008)

STEVEN SEBRING

You wanna film me? Patti Smith says.

Yeah, says Steven.

What for?

To see who you really are. To see what you do and how you do it. To understand you, Patti.

You wanna cut me up into tiny pieces and sew the parts together? she says. If you film the outside, what about my insides? If I explain my inner thoughts to you, everything will come out, you see. Can you really communicate another person by showing them walking into the shower, or humming tunes, or eating dinner, or sharing memories? You'll try to tell a story but there is no story. Wouldn't it be a trick? I am right here, man. I'm growing old. So are my kids. So are you. This is the only thing I know. I don't need to be remembered. It's all in the art I produce.

She shakes his hand, thanks him for his time, and walks out the door. Steven waits for the 'I'm sorry, but' speech from Lenny Kaye, but Lenny smiles and says, We'll see you next week.

17

In the grounds of the Detroit Institute of Arts, Michael Heizer, sitting in the cabin of a tractor, waves his cowboy hat and lassoes the air whilst dragging a thirty-ton granite slab over the manicured lawn.

This is *Dragged Mass*.

The commission is a breakthrough, a way to get things moving here, rip apart the marbled hallways and the monotony of the established art scene. The torn gulley that scars the lawn and the heavy weight of mass symbolize the necessary destruction of old order.

The curator Sam Wagstaff welcomes it with a loving embrace.

The mass sits there for days. Rain falls. The buckled gulley becomes a muddy trench. The mass, which is supposed to sink majestically into the lawn, does not sink. Eventually, it is hauled away, blown up with dynamite and removed piece by piece.

In New York City, Sam tours the downtown galleries during the day. At night he tours the bars and clubs. This is a contrast from the world he's left behind, the perfect green lawn (restored at great expense), the empty hallways and reverent air. There, his body was just an empty ancient vessel. Here, he can touch things, feel their weight.

—

The first time Sam Wagstaff sees Robert Mapplethorpe is in a photograph on the mantelpiece of a mutual friend. In the picture, Robert, dressed in a French sailor hat, is smiling coyly at the camera.

Who is this? says Sam.

Robert Mapplethorpe.

The feeling in his stomach is the same as when he looks at a great work of art.

The first time Sam speaks to Robert on the telephone he says, I'm looking for someone to spoil. And Robert says, You've found him.

The first time Sam visits Robert's studio, he sees a pair of leather pants hanging on the wall with a baguette protruding at the crotch.

The first time Sam meets Patti, she is barely dressed. Her hair a mess, she speaks in sweet profanities.

The first thing Sam buys Robert is a camera. The second is an apartment far away from Patti.

Sam tells Robert to take more photographs. They go away together to Fire Island, to European cities. Robert takes photographs of Sam as he used to take photographs of other people. Sam doesn't mind – it is the *way* Robert takes the photographs.

Sam becomes the subject of art. In Robert's photographs, Sam is dressed or not dressed at all. Sam in the bath, pulling faces in repose, a man preparing himself for the day; at the beach, in a dark room, dressed in nothing but a pair of white underpants. There are the couple shots – artist and patron – Sam squatting in the corner of a white room and Robert standing over him, one arm over his head, Robert, the skinny kid in loose denim jeans; the wedding picture, Sam in front of Robert though it is always Robert's face you're drawn towards; images spread across the pages of a photo album, four eight-panel pages showing a cock bound and trussed in black leather cord – Sam's or Robert's, it's not entirely clear – cord tied between the buttocks, twisted and fastened to the wrists, the front view, back view, side view.

Before Robert, Sam didn't consider photographs to be works of art. They were more like historical documentation or reportage to him. It is Robert Mapplethorpe who changes his mind. Sam sees Edward Steichen's *Flatiron Building* like the prow of a ship emerging through the mist, the dagger-sharp blackness of the tree branch cutting through the rain-drenched air.

It looks just like a painting, he says. Not like a photograph at all.

And there is that feeling again: the turning of his stomach.

Sam Wagstaff buys the photographs in auction houses and in second-hand stores. A long line of people form quickly behind him. The crowd picks up the pictures that Sam has been looking at. They want to see what Sam has seen. Sam and Robert carry the photographs back to Sam's apartment in plastic bags and brown-paper bags. Patti comes later to organize the pictures. She lays the photographs out on the floor and orders them, catalogues them, figures out where they should go.

Robert and Sam enjoy the thrill of the chase. But once they possess the item, it loses its meaning.

For Sam, the subject of the photograph is not important. It could be of anything – medical photographs from the turn of the century, industrial photographs from the 1930s, anonymous photographs from any time at all. What Sam does is bring them all together so that a person can look at one and then another in one view. In their mind there will form a sequence, something of Sam's imagination displayed in a line.

At an exhibition of his own photography collection, Sam reads the words from the exhibition catalogue: *This exhibition is about pleasure, the pleasure of looking and the pleasure of seeing, like watching people dancing through an open window. They seem a little mad at first, until you realize they hear the song that you are watching.*

Sam's favourite photograph in the exhibition is Thomas Eakins' *Male Nudes: Students at a Swimming Hole, 1883.* The picture shows a group of naked young men. Two are swimming in a lake, one is sitting on the bank, two are gazing into the water, two are getting ready to jump. One is cocked and ready, balanced on the edge of a rock, about to dive. Sam feels as though he comes to the scene by accident, strolling through a wood, the last days of summer, when the season has cooled, when the air has changed, when the day seems shorter than it should. The diver holds his position. His friends look on, frozen in time. A breeze blows in, not one of them moves. Water laps their skin. A beetle crawls across the diver's toe. The sun shimmers on the water, catches the surface, catches the eye.

When Sam looks at the photograph he feels the simple joy of witnessing something beautiful. These boys remain fixed. They won't swim away. They will never grow old.

The other photographs depict the American wilderness – Niagara Falls, the Nevada desert, the beginnings of a Western railroad, working-class portraits, medical experiments, industrial scenes. The spectacle of a hippopotamus stuck behind bars with children looking on, geese flying low over an ocean, Lewis Carroll's *Girl on Sofa*, coy and perverse in the way she bends her knee and looks at the camera, knowing much more than she should. The madness of Boulogne's *Fright Mixed with Pain, Torture* – the woman's face seized with electrical pulses, *President Lincoln on the battlefield of Antietam, Fifth Avenue at Rush Hour*.

And here are Robert's photographs:

Jim and Tom, Sausalito, 1977, the leather-clad gimp pissing into another man's mouth, the arch of urine, suspended in mid-air, the warm, fleshy mouth, which eternally

81

holds the piss, dark shadows, sharp against a sun-bleached wall, a streak of sunlight reflecting off leather, the men standing and kneeling, suspended. And Robert's *Tulips, New York, 1977*, freshly cut, positioned in a vase, straight and true, except one, drooping off to the side.

Sam doesn't know why he collects the way he does. He says that an obsession – like any sort of love – is blinding.

The camera observes and records passively, without intrusion, and yet it makes an argument by organizing subjects into a two-dimensional plane within which Sam is made to understand.

Robert says that when he takes a photograph or when he has sex he disappears. Like when you are the artist or when you are the art itself, the focal point of everything, you cease to exist.

Sam looks for Robert in the tulip heads, the erect stalks, the black background, but there is only his own reflection in the glass.

When Sam's mother dies, Robert is away in London. Sam sits beside her bed and takes her photograph. He photographs her face and her hands. He photographs the bed frame and the bedspread. He photographs the bedside table, her reading glasses, water glass, a vase containing roses. He photographs the view from her window and the way the curtains are tied. He photographs the paintings on the wall, the dressing gown hanging on the door, her slippers under the bed. The pictures will preserve a silence that doesn't exist in reality, for there is noise coming in through the open window – traffic, glass bottles being dumped upon the sidewalk. He can hear his own heart beating and he can feel a nervous twitch in his knee that pauses only when he stops to take a photograph. He takes more pictures. He thinks, If I can't understand this thing for what it is, I'll understand it in pieces. Then he thinks, Now that she is dead, Robert will have to come home for the funeral.

Sam sets up the studio – white walls, bright lights: these photographs will be in colour. Patti, in a good mood, sits on the floor, tosses the feather boa over her shoulder and picks up the kitten. She laughs at Sam, who is watching her. She repositions her hat and holds up the kitten. She looks at the camera and smiles. Sam takes her picture.

When Robert finds out he is very, very angry. He yells at Sam, Don't you know who we are? I AM THE ARTIST AND YOU ARE THE COLLECTOR! Sam and Patti feel very guilty. All the pictures belong to Robert, the master of their universe.

Robert decorates his Bond Street studio. He paints the walls and floorboards black, creates a giant cage out of chicken wire, places his bed in the centre. He works how he lives. This building used to house a factory but now it is filled with art. It is all about money, art, love and rent, all things are up for exchange – this is something Sam always says to Robert – remember who pays your rent.

———

Robert doesn't always remember. He telephones Sam and lists all of the men he has been with and all of the places he has gone. He lists his collection of physical symptoms – tiredness, back pain, groin strain, lice, rashes, swellings. As he speaks, Sam imagines him twirling the phone cord around his fingers like a debutante and thinks, That's me being wrapped around his little finger.

Jim Nelson arrives in the overnight delivery (a gift from Robert, who is in San Francisco). He is slim, attractive and new to New York. Sam buys himself a home on Long Island. At weekends and in between shows Sam and Jim rest up here and feel very grand. One thing Jim wants to do is grow wild roses. Sam doesn't mind, except, when he thinks about the roses, he thinks about Robert's photographs of flowers. Wherever Jim decides to try to plant the roses they just don't grow. He tries them in a sunny spot and then a shady spot. He tries them by the perimeter wall and by the exterior wall of the house. He plants them too close to the woodland and wild deer eat the bushes before anything can grow. All the time they are in Manhattan, Jim can only think of the roses. He talks about them all the time to Sam. Jim is a hairdresser by trade. He has spent his adult life cutting things back but now the roses won't grow.

When Sam's photography collection is complete he sells it to the Getty Museum for five million dollars. His critics say that this is self-sabotage. They say it is the action of a man who wants to build something up until he loves it so much he cannot help but despise it. They say the collection represents him, and he is the thing he has come to despise.

Sam starts to collect American silver. He raids the salerooms and the auction rooms. He drags it all back to his place in black plastic sacks. He stands on the Long Island beach and scours the sand for remains of ancient shipwrecks, shoes off, wading through the soft sand, feeling for shards of silver with his bare feet. He finds pottery shards and polishes them. He commissions an artist to make them into jewellery. He does not stop looking until it is night time, and, even then, once he is back inside the house, he is looking out at the beach imagining the silver.

His critics say that this collecting of silver is a sign of early dementia – a Polish émigré wanting to possess more silverware than the Boston museum. Others say this is just an example of his capacity to love.

Robert comes to visit Sam in hospital but he cannot look at Sam. Sam is dying. He is no longer beautiful. AIDS has eaten away his body. His is thin and grey. His eyes are sunken. He has become an ancient, empty vessel. Sam is finding it hard to speak but he manages to say to Patti: *If you want any of my money be nice to Robert because I'm giving him everything.*

—

Sam's body is placed in the Wagstaff family crypt. He was a collector of art for so long and then he was the subject of art, and then he was the subject of history.

Robert Mapplethorpe's photograph of Sam Wagstaff shows him staring defiantly into the distance. His neck muscles are taut. The area around his head is illuminated with light like a halo, and that makes the rest of his figure appear more definite. He is very beautiful. He has a strong jaw and forehead. He is solid and weighty, like a statue or a monument.

18

Edmund White follows the assistant down the carpeted corridor of the Midtown office tower. The building is a dreary sequence of office cubicles, walls covered in an array of personal effects: family photos, holiday photos, notes and calendars, sheets of white paper. Midtown and the Empire State Building are visible through exterior windows. They look grave and unmanageably high. Manuscripts reflect the towers outside, piled high on every desk, higher than the workers sitting there who are doubled over the print, shoulders hunched, the murmur of voices, telephone trills, stacks of cardboard boxes, taller than Edmund.

Edmund's editor shakes him by the hand. He could be in his twenties, thirties or forties. He has a universally appropriate smile. He is always pleased to see Edmund White. His handshake is firm and vigorous. Edmund is asked to sit in his office. An assistant hands Edmund a cup of coffee for which he has not asked.

Good to be back on track, hey, Ed? says his editor. We just love what you're doing with the book. He pats the manuscript on the desk.

Edmund knows he won't use any of those scenes. He has been trying to write about the Painted Boy, an update to the original story. It is supposed to be about the Painted

Boy in modern times. It's not as straightforward as he originally thought. Every time he describes the boy he thinks of himself. He no longer wants to write about himself. He wants to think about the future. But Edmund feels very tired. He wants to write about New York. He cannot tell his editor this.

Edmund wipes his brow with the back of his hand. The coffee they have given him is very pale.

The assistant leans over and places her hand on Edmund's arm.

You must be very tired, she says.

Her fingers are very cold. She can't be more than twenty-two.

The editor taps the end of his pencil against the edge of his desk.

You seem concerned, Edmund, he says. What's wrong? Why not take the afternoon off. Go see friends. Go have some fun.

Edmund remembers the Hudson River piers where he loved strangers in the dark. Unemployment was high in the city then. On sunny days men sat outside and dangled their legs above the Hudson. They bathed in the sun. They lay out.

Returning to what is now the Hudson River Park, the space he finds is a long strip of manicured lawn. Cycle lanes stretch north and south. Joggers speed past. Their elasticated clothing is a multi-coloured blur. Edmund is standing with his back to the expressway. He is stuck between the rush of vehicular traffic and speeding exercisers. He is waiting for his moment to cross.

He does not find the structures he remembers. He is looking at the high-rise shore of New Jersey but he remembers danger, abandonment and the exchange of love. He remembers the rude dark. In the summer, when the sun was bright, it seemed a greater leap of faith to step foot inside those piers, for one step took you into blackness. Knife-sharp walls of light streamed in through injured ceilings. He loved the glory holes, the contextless dicks suspended in the wall. He loved to get onto his knees.

He remembers the backwards nature of time when the moon was the noontime sun and walks were midday strolls in the dead of night.

His favourite places were ordinary restrooms, alleyways, trucks, parks, subway stations. The men who used these places were ordinary people. He chose hustlers who were physically imperfect. To go with an Adonis just wasn't realistic. There had to be an element of reality about it. It couldn't be pure fantasy. It had to be authentic. A worn, imperfect body was a body with a past. It was into the grooves of history that he placed his desires.

He used to wait in the piers when it was dark. He was frightened. But that was the point – you didn't know what would happen. There had been murders, muggings, people took advantage, but this made Edmund feel alive. He waited in the dark. He could hear the lapping of the river against the posts, the repetitive slap of waves rebounding off passing ships.

He remembers the vast internal space, the piers occupied by them. The piers were dilapidated, sure, but they were used.

After a while he'd see somebody. They'd both be a little suspicious. Maybe he'd like the look of him and maybe he wouldn't, but in the end there was always someone. Edmund would find a place – perhaps he'd do it right there in the middle of the cavernous shell where their voices echoed and other men crowded to see. Or maybe they'd go off and find somewhere private. Or if it was sunny, perhaps they'd go out onto the deck and find a warm spot and do it there, outside, on the boardwalk, with only the Hudson beside them and the passing ships. It was exciting, not knowing how the story would end.

And afterwards they would maybe share a smoke or go their separate ways, or else Edmund would hang around and watch the boats go by. Edmund could never leave. He had to see what the next ten minutes would bring.

Edmund walks to the Chelsea Piers. These are a series of industrial units containing sports facilities and conference spaces. Edmund White could enter now and play ice hockey. He could play soccer or ten-pin bowling. He could play basketball. He could do all manner of things that require the adding up of numbers, points, watching scores accumulate, lit beneath artificially brilliant light, move his body to the limits of physical endurance. He could become a physical creature again. He could count the seconds, time, as he used to. He could run on a treadmill or ride a stationary bike. But what would be the point of this? Why run on a machine when you can fuck?

19

In 1939, Moses tries to build a bridge across New York Bay, connecting the Battery with Brooklyn.

This bridge will cross infamous water. It will be more magnificent than Brooklyn Bridge. As a consequence the city will lose Battery Park, but this is a necessary sacrifice.

But Moses, although powerful, is not God. He cannot just click his fingers and have his own way. It seems that the public love Battery Park and they are willing to fight for it. They love seeing the Statue of Liberty and Governors Island. Those who work in the offices on Wall Street like a calm place to stretch their legs. The workers in the fish markets of South Street come here to get out of the crowds, throw a line in and wait for a catch. The idea of an imposing structure like a bridge cutting across the bay is obscene. It is as if they can all remember sailing into New York on immigrant ships, fresh from Ellis Island, the famous New York skyline before them. To have a bridge here blocking the view of the city is more grotesque than anyone can bear. To destroy Battery Park and Castles Clinton where the great singer Jenny Lind once sang!

Moses is ordered to build a tunnel instead. But a tunnel to

Moses is just a hole in the ground. There is no point in building something no one can see.

He thinks, If they want a tunnel then that's what they'll get. But they'll get other things besides.

He announces that the construction of a tunnel directly beneath Castle Clinton will weaken the structure, making the Aquarium there unsafe. So he evacuates the fish. The lights are switched off. The pumps are disconnected. The display cases are dismantled and scrapped. The castle stands empty.

Next, he tells the city that Castle Clinton is in need of structural repair, and as there is not enough money to pay for this, the castle will have to be demolished. He is not sentimental about the past. The past is nothing but a distraction of time. He orders a high wall to be built around Castle Clinton.

Campaigners fight to save the castle. They persuade the National Park Service to take it over. The castle is saved; the public have won! But Moses tells them they are too late for he has already knocked their castle down. He tells them that it's gone, it's all over. He says, You were the ones who wanted a tunnel. They all believe Moses – City Hall, the press. But one member of the public doesn't. This man demands the key to the gate at Castle Clinton. He storms down there and lets himself in. He climbs over the pile of debris and sees the castle, standing as it has always stood, solid, permanent.

Eventually, the Brooklyn–Battery Tunnel is built. For Moses, nothing at all has changed. Castle Clinton is left untouched. Traffic travels underground. Nothing can be seen by anyone. There are no visible changes here. The Battery remains the same and life goes on as it did before. No one is seen to be moving anywhere. A public work that remains invisible is just a waste of money.

Piers

(1975–86)

ALVIN BALTROP

Two men are standing in a derelict room amidst broken floorboards before three glassless windows. One man is crouching down, sucking the other man's dick. His hand is pressed into the buttock of the other man. The other man is holding him by the shoulders and bending over, his curly hair hanging down.

Two men are lying naked side by side on the ground. The sun is streaming across their bodies. They are touching each other, a hand on a shoulder, a finger on a mouth. Their dicks are pointing towards one another as if engaged in conversation.

Three naked men are outside in the sunshine. One is lying on his front, legs spread. Another is sitting with his back to the camera. The last is standing with a leg perched on a wooden pylon, his buttocks large and round in the sun. He is wearing black plimsolls and white socks. The interior of the pier is black.

Many men are lined up along the pier, which has a large

gash in its wall. Their bare legs hang over the Hudson. They are sharing conversation, sitting out in the sun.

A pier has deteriorated. Its outer shell is warped into undulations. Its shape reflects the choppy water beneath it.

A pier is an expansive white box. Manhattan looms in the distance, large and black. Two figures are standing on the pier, one bent over, the other behind.

A man, naked from the waist down, stands on a bollard and looks into the pier through a broken window.

A police boat is pulled up against the pier and tied there. Cops are standing around a naked corpse. The back of the corpse is marked with deep lacerations. Pulled freshly from the Hudson.

20

There is nothing compared to the feeling of being able to lie on a floor that you have laid yourself, says Walt. Covered over by a ceiling fitted by your own hands. The places where we live shape us, Bucke. My family and I built houses in Brooklyn. We marked out the plots and laid the foundations. We nailed in every plank of wood and secured every window. In many ways, building a house is the same as making a book. Many parts are added together to form a whole, and people live within both. I am a poet and a builder. In my experience, land developers and publishers always want to raise the devil and break things apart. They want to manipulate creation but, despite this, I have continued to build many houses and write many poems.

Bucke's eyes have not yet grown accustomed to the dark. As a child, Bucke longed to die just to see what would happen. Would there be a God? He imagined there would be nothing. Not even consciousness left.

Splitting

(1974)

GORDON MATTA-CLARK

Gordon Matta-Clark has sawn through a wooden-framed house in New Jersey, splitting it in two.

The two halves of the house are leaning and separate.

Sunlight shines through the split.

The sky is visible through the split in the banister, floor and ceiling.

Rooms are separated by the split.

His friends come to visit him from New York. They park their van in an adjacent field and laugh about how far away they are.

What do your neighbours say? his friend says.

They say it's about society pulling apart, he says.

I'm starving, she says. Do you have a kitchen? Or has the stove been cut in two?

Gordon likes the view from the top of the house. Standing on the roof and leaning as the roof leans, he looks out over the land. He feels good standing on this roof, but it is not New York. When he is in New York he walks all over the city. There, he stands flat-footed on the ground. The architectural rupture of that place at this time is greater than anything he can accomplish here.

21

You know, you should get a tattoo, says Robert Mapplethorpe.

I already have one, the man says.

Oh yeah? Where?

The man smiles.

I should have guessed, says Robert. Now turn around.

The man does what he's told.

Robert moves the camera. He repositions the lamp. He takes a photograph.

I'm gonna use a whole roll, Robert says.

He takes more photographs.

Now just stand straight and tall. Look right into the camera. Don't move, Robert says.

Robert has transformed his studio into a living-room scene with a comfortable armchair and a table lamp, a mantelpiece with ornaments, a side table with deer antler legs.

The couple come in full leather gear, wearing chains and reins. They stand and sit. The man who is shackled at the wrists and ankles is sitting in the chair, his hands on his lap. His bearded partner is standing beside him, holding the reins and a riding crop. Their shadows loom on the wall behind them. Outside it is night. They look at the camera.

—

Robert's leather portfolio includes: the glint of a dog collar and a leather jacket. A close-up of a genital pouch. *Ramsey, New York, 1979* – black man, leather vest, penis out. Cock in a vice, nail hammered into the end. Next, all the blood resulting from this. The man's fingernails are cut short and grubby. A laughing devil mask is positioned beside it. *Two Men Ass Sucking, 1979.* Face with a boot. Clothes-peg mouth: pegs secured to the top and bottom lips then fanned out. Gimps, cowboy, a man reclining. *White male / bearded / kneeling on zebra bedspread / blinds in back / tattoo on arm (double | symbol) nipple ring, tear on.* The man is pudgy and kneeling, leather trousers, his tongue is out. *Richard, 1978,* bloody cock on torture board with mask. *Cock – penis/balls hanging out of white leather, 1981. Unidentified / Ass / Man facing backwards on toilet jock strap on, 1979. Ron Stevenson, Shaved Ass, 1978. Dominic and Elliot – grabbing cock and balls, 1979. Charles and Jim Freeman, 1976* – lunging in for a kiss and the chair is tipping. *Jim and Tom Sausalito, 1977 / kneeling mouth open, no pee.* The finger enters the head of the penis – *Lou, NYC, 1978, similar to map184/ finger in penis hole.* Knife in cock (the cock is fake). Muscle man dressed up in fishnets and bra, eyeliner, curly hair. He is sitting down and protecting his private parts.

In Floral Park, Harry Mapplethorpe looks out of his kitchen window. The front lawn is at least two inches longer than that of the neighbours. It is spreading into the flowerbeds.

Harry sips his coffee and lights a cigarette. His friend is coming up the path.

Your grass is getting long out there, his friend says.

Just thinking the same thing, says Harry.

I took a trip into the city last week, Harry. I went to see Robert's exhibition.

Harry looks out at the overgrown lawn.

I don't know, Harry, I'm no expert, but there's something seriously wrong with that kid.

The Flatiron

(1904)

EDWARD J. STEICHEN

The Flatiron Building emerges through the mist. The prow. A glorious ship coming to a rest. As beautiful as any painting.

22

If Edmund wants to write about New York he must try not to yearn for what is no longer there. But it is difficult to leave the past alone.

When Edmund wrote *The Joy of Gay Sex* he talked to all the men he knew and asked them about their lives and sexual preferences. He asked them what worried them the most. He talked to doctors and professionals. He asked them the risks and dangers of particular acts. He asked them what techniques they knew to be safe. He organized the information in an a–z list and wrote a paragraph on each – *Anus*, *Blow Job*, *Body Image*. Whenever Edmund grew tired of writing he made himself imagine the young boy sitting alone in his bedroom, looking out across the pastures of his family's farm, confused by his emotions, without a friend in the world, without any guidance, containing desires, feeling afraid. Edmund thought about this lonely boy and he thought about himself. What if this boy could read Edmund's book and finally understand that he was not alone?

Edmund sat in his New York apartment and he wrote alone. He wrote about sex on the street. He imagined it happening beneath his window. He imagined it filling up the city. He worked very hard on the book. He worked so hard that in order to have the time to write about sex he had to give up the sex. He was left with words only. He became a symbol of sexuality instead of a man. The writing, although enjoyable, could never replace the physical act. I am a man, he thought. I am made of flesh and blood.

Edmund takes the notebooks from his desk. He rips out the pages and lays them on the floor.

I remember when the city was different, not clean but fuggy, filthy.

The city, as it was then, was broken, on its knees, on the edge of disaster, and in many ways so was I.

He witnessed the birth of sexual revolution. Here it lies across the apartment floor on pages of unlined white paper, their edges scored and jagged from extraction, their edges ripped and torn from the hurry of wanting to put it all into place.

The man in the apartment across the street is watering his plants. He tips his whole body forward as he performs this act. He is wearing just a singlet because of the heat. He seems very old. His body is stiff. The movement of his tipping over is not smooth and continuous but a series of awkward individual labours.

Edmund pulls his books from the shelves and scans the pages for information. He wrote these passages himself but now they make no sense to him.

He switches on the television. A news feature shows a pretty woman standing on the steps of the Tenement Museum in the Lower East Side of New York. Men, women and children are standing beside her in old-fashioned dress, self-consciously not looking at the camera – *This is how it used to be – this is where we come from, from the Lower East Side where workers of this city built the industrial foundations on which we have secured a comfortable future –*

He switches channel.

Eyes closed, grip, hard, intense, clutching. The man is red all over from exertion, he pushes, pushes. His partner is mute, trussed up, silenced with a gag, fellated and assaulted. This is ridiculous, yet Edmund watches.

Edmund is finding it hard to imagine.

Edmund sees life in bright flashes. These disjointed scenes come to him on a rolling film but with each vignette he has missed the titles and the set-up of the drama and he cannot get a handle on the plot. These are individual flashes of things he has seen or things he has invented – he isn't sure which – he cannot remember – two men fucking in the corner of a dark club, right at the beginning of liberation. He watched two men in the dim candlelight and he thought the scene looked so romantic. It meant that things were changing, didn't it? He was fresh back from Europe where everything was old.

He picks up *The Joy of Gay Sex.*

If you have trouble swallowing him whole, try it in the morning when the gag reflex is weaker.

And:

Old age is the unspoken horror of homosexuality. It is said that to grow old is a death sentence, but true love knows no boundaries. True love sees past things like age. If you love someone, age doesn't matter. There are many physical pleasures to be had at any age, even if you are old.

23

Jane Jacobs is sitting at the window of her Hudson Street apartment in 1959. She is watching her neighbours sitting on stoops in the sun. They are sharing beers and lying back. Kids sketch hopscotch grids on the ground before them. As the sun drifts down the street, the kids drift with it. After an hour they are playing down the street. They join other kids sitting on the stoop there. Out comes a skipping rope, and this game takes over. Their skipping routines are fast and elaborate. They begin to attract a crowd of passers-by. When they are finished they bow to their audience. The crowd applauds and moves on. The children produce a deck of cards. They sit on the ground and deal out the cards.

This kind of thing happens all the time here. Children play in the street instead of the park because they want to be where the action is. Her own son likes to play in the street. He uses the narrow gap between two buildings as a safe place to store his treasured possessions: his tennis balls, his comic books. This space is his den, his hollow tree. Jane is happy to let him do this because her neighbours are watching from their stoops. Everyone is watching the streets. This is how New York works.

But residents are being cleared off the streets to make way for traffic, and Jane is worried. She knows that when the city planner looks down from his high tower he does not see a community; he sees only buildings blocking his way. To him, a city is just a problem to be solved. Jane thinks that the growth of a city should be slow and organic, its development as natural as the growth of a leaf.

She closes her notebook and sits back. In her mind is an image of an empty city. She sketches the outline of Manhattan Island on the cover of her notebook – a diagram devoid of life.

24

Everyone is watching Bucke and Whitman as they walk through the dining car. Of course, they recognize Whitman. Or perhaps it is because Walt is wearing no overshirt, which is his custom on vacations. Bucke supposes this is all it is for him, just a vacation on a train.

Their accommodation is basic, a private room with two bench seats over which, at night time, are suspended two sleeping hammocks. While Bucke and Whitman are eating dinner, someone comes to hang and furnish the beds. While they are eating breakfast someone folds the beds away. Walt wants to know who performs these tasks. Bucke explains that the porter must do it. As soon as they sit down to eat, Walt dashes off. He returns an hour later. You were right, he says. There is a man who does it.

Bucke is struck by the darkness, the fading light. No one yet has come to light the lamps. A shadow has fallen across Whitman's face. The sky is a darkening blue.

Tell me about the war, Bucke says.

It is through war that we understand our true capacity to love, says Walt. After witnessing horror one is filled with such an energy and sense of being alive – love spills from you – and something is formed from this. It is like building something very tall and wide. It is like building something

109

that fills all space. You feel you could live for ever because the truth of it is that your body will not.

I love my brother very much, says Walt. And I loved the soldiers. When I saw the soldiers in that camp, I loved them more because they were all my brother. Love includes all things and all people, Bucke.

I spent many nights in the camp. I wrote out letters for the soldiers. They told me great stories of their youth. There were many soldiers from Brooklyn and Long Island. Their past became my past, and mine theirs. I sat beside them as they lay dying. The light was darkening in my eyes too. The blood that ran through my veins and spilled from theirs was the same. The sound of the men, the groans and screams, laughter too, was the same. All people who are and who have ever lived and who would ever live existed in that tent. I slept in their beds. When they died I died. I have died more than a thousand times through my connection with these men, yet I continue to live. This is how I know that life is eternal. Other people will continue to live even when I don't. The light has grown dim, hasn't it, Bucke? We are sitting in darkness.

Day's End

(1975)

GORDON MATTA-CLARK

The interior of a Hudson River pier is a vast space. Shafts
of light cut through the darkness, streaming in through
openings in the roof. The Hudson is visible through holes
in the floor.

25

Back home in Jackson, Tennessee, Milton Moore knew his place. He was anonymous, his family large, his future uncertain. He looked for other places to go. Eventually, exchanging one confinement for another, he joined the US Navy. He sailed the ocean on a ship filled with men. He dutifully wore his uniform. He manned and scrubbed the deck. He drilled and followed orders, not knowing who the hell he was. He bided his time waiting for the ship to dock, and made his escape through the Hudson River piers.

Now, Milton is swept along on a brand-new tide, the surf of 42nd Street. He passes the men who holler the plots of movies outside the movie houses. Bright posters depict oiled and bronzed women shrieking in horror, fear, desire, their mouths are wide open, red, black hollows for throats, heaving chests, long legs, nails. Men grimace in the cold: the taut lines of their faces crack. Raw hands clutch admission tickets. He looks at the hang-low, slung-back featureless faces of boys too young to know any better.

Milton passes through the movie lines, breaks the crowd apart, cuts through the laugh and talk, the steamy breath of strangers intent on looking. The movie is about to begin. They wave dollar bills, a mere formality for the night they will have, their bodies sitting in a dark room filled with other bodies, watching bodies fucking on a screen. Milton is not inconspicuous here. He stands right out. Predators look. They do it quickly, clocking this guy then that guy. Milton is both the competition and the prize. On this street, he walks a little taller.

Milton stops for a drink in a dive bar, fresh off the ship, hot off the press. Men try on his hat. Men reach for his uniform, the space where medals should go. The bar is very loud. He cannot distinguish music from speech. He walks through to the back of the bar and into the restroom. He catches his reflection in the mirror. His suit is already sullied and ridiculous, this white uniform with this black body underneath. The guy at the urinal looks a second too long. Milton locks himself into a stall. He climbs on the toilet bowl and pushes the window open. He shifts and shimmies out.

Milton sticks to the dark side of the street, walks east. He throws away his hat and his medalless coat. He wants it all to fall away from him, the whole of him. He walks all night and all day. He thinks: Milton Moore was born. One day he was produced. His hands are the same. His heart and his head are the same. They have not been exchanged. This is the body he will have for the rest of his life.

Milton hangs out at a bar on West Street in the Village where he enjoys the closely pressed bodies, which obscure

113

his own, the loud music and low light. The men there are shadows, nothing more, and the drinks are cheap. One night, after leaving the bar, as he is walking down the street, he hears footsteps running in his direction. He quickens his pace, hurries towards the subway.

Wait! a voice calls. Wait!

He glances over his shoulder and sees a slim white man wearing a black leather jacket running after him, waving his arms in the air.

Wait! the man shouts again, and Milton stops.

The man halts and tries to catch his breath.

Please, he says. I'm Robert Mapplethorpe. I'm a photographer. I think you're perfect.

Back at Robert's studio, Milton strips.

Milton is perfectly in proportion, ribbed, tight torso, hard muscles, gigantic cock hanging there, partly erect.

Milton is nervous.

He is cold. The coldness only extenuates the hardness of his muscles. His nipples are hard. His cock is getting harder.

How would you like it if I photographed you? Robert says.

Robert takes a photograph of his head and his chest, his dick, his ass, and his hands.

Do you still have your uniform?

Milton shakes his head.

Robert tosses him another. He wears it for Robert. Then

he takes it off, garment by garment, exposing himself in parts.

I don't want my face and my body to be photographed at the same time, says Milton. I don't want it to get back to my parents; I don't want them to see.

So Robert will never show Milton's face and his body in the same photograph and he will never tell anyone his name. From now on, Milton is never Milton, just a list of body parts.

Milton soon develops habits. He writes complex words on his hands in black marker pen. When he has covered his left palm, he covers his right. Robert doesn't like it. He says it's like being rubbed down with the inside of a book. He gets Milton to clean his hands before they do it, but sometimes he doesn't. There is also the handwriting, the awkward, childlike scrawl, which Robert hates, though it is no worse than his.

Robert introduces Milton at parties but it is clear these people cannot understand why Robert is with a man like Milton because Milton is not articulate and he is not very charming.

Robert says he mustn't worry. This is not an English lesson. He is not a school kid. This is not a test. Milton doesn't think this is true. Everything is school. Everything is a test.

———

When Robert goes away he locks Milton in the apartment. A man called Edmund comes to check on him. Milton pours him a drink. Edmund tips his glass and asks him questions. Milton thinks he is a psychiatrist, the way he talks and tips his drink, but he says he is a writer. He asks if Milton has ever read anything by him and Milton says no. Edmund walks over to the bookcase and pulls a book down from the shelf. He looks at the spine then flicks through its pages. Milton rubs the palm of his hand on the couch, scrubs the words off. Suddenly, they seem absurd.

Milton sees his own reflection in the fishes and the vases of Robert's glass collection. His face is distorted in bulges and elongations. He is black, green, blue. He is the head of the fish and the body and the tail. What else is he supposed to do all day? Robert has told him to stay inside. He looks at the glass. Milton surveys the room. It is a fucking museum. Here is the picture, *Man in Polyester Suit*. A cheap grey suit with matching vest and a white shirt. The man's stance is active. He looks like he is strolling somewhere. His fly is undone and his cock is sticking out. The long vein that extends down the black shaft is the only part that really seems alive.

Milton cannot get out of Robert's apartment. The door is locked and bolted on the outside. He presses his body against the door as if his body will again provide the answer. He shoulders the door. He studies the smudged words on his hands. He presses them against the door. He tries the handle but the door is locked. He looks at the glass collection for an answer. He is trapped. He is surrounded by glass too precious to break, much more precious than him.

Milton opens the window and climbs down the fire escape. He runs all the way to the Hudson. He stands there on the edge of the abandoned pier looking into the black water, the swirls and eddies, the random movement of the water against the posts, hurried and frenetic. He jumps in. The water is warm. Forever the sailor, he swims to New Jersey.

26

Edmund White is standing in the huddle on the sidewalk, sheltering from the rain under the awning of an executive midtown hotel. He is forced along the sidewalk by the crowd and forced down the slippery subway steps, through the ticket barrier, down the escalator. He enters a long tiled tunnel where a man is playing a saxophone. He presses himself against the wall. Music echoes in this underground chamber. He sees a mosaic depicting the roots of a tree plunging down from the ceiling. The brown roots reach outwards. Beside the mosaic are the words of Goethe – 'The unnatural – that too is natural'.

Oh God.

He remembers.

The club lay buried deep underground. The deeper he descended, the more it resembled his subconscious. The floor was sticky with drying blood and semen. He wore nothing but his shoes. Men were phantoms in the dark. Rooms were furnished with slings for fisting, meat blocks, chains and whips. Rooms were divided into separate cubicles. Here was one room. Here was another. Here was one body. Here was another. Each room and each body had its own place there. Every space was filled to its internal limit. He wandered through the busy corridors. These men were no more real to him than the dreams he had at

118

night. He passed displays of dicks. As whole men they were unreachable but the individual segments of their bodies were OK – he could deal with parts. The dick was the part he wanted most. It does not represent anything else.

Memorial
(2001)

The photographs appear all over the city. Where one is posted, hundreds soon follow. They are stuck onto lamp-posts, fences and walls. They are protected from the rain by plastic wallets. Despite this precaution, the rain has turned the bold ink into cascading rivers. Each poster displays a collection of individual instances. There is the instant the person was last seen alive, and the instant of the first collision, the instant of the second collision, the instant of the first fall, and the instant of the second fall, the instant of the rescue, the instant the rescue was over and the instant the rescue became a recovery.

27

From 1941 right through to the '60s, Robert Moses wants to build the Lower Manhattan Expressway, a ten-lane elevated road over Broome Street in the Lower East Side, built forty feet above the ground. It will link the Holland Tunnel on the west side of Manhattan with the Williamsburg Bridge on the east. A branch will separate south along Mott Street, across Canal, and connect to the Manhattan Bridge, cutting through SoHo and Little Italy.

Moses says this is the only way to ease congestion. Manhattan is missing vital cross-town roads. Streets like Spring, Prince and Bond have had their day. The factory buildings there are no longer used. The Lower East Side is a slum where the children play out in the streets. Better to build new housing blocks on the outskirts of the city, build gardens and playgrounds, move these people out.

Jane Jacobs storms down Broome Street with fliers in her hand. She points to the elegant cast-iron buildings and describes in detail to passers-by the intricate mouldings and the history of its inhabitants – all this will be lost, she says, and all for a highway. The homes and businesses you see around you will disappear. We will lose our city. Is this what you want?

—

She arranges to meet an artist on the corner of the Bowery and East Houston Street.

As they walk through the neighbourhood, up the Bowery, across Bond Street, Jane is thinking: Let the businesses reflect the local community. Let the blocks be short and low. Improve public transportation. Stop people from getting into their cars. Listen to the women who live in this city. They are the ones who understand how it works.

She looks around her and imagines industrial workers going in and coming out through the heavy factory doors, the grind of machines, soot-heavy, rank air. Today, a different activity has taken its place.

The artist explains what's going on.

We've made improvements to the interior spaces, she says. We've installed plumbing and electrics, redecorated, fixed elevator shafts and air-conditioning units. We've reconstructed doors, rebuilt partition walls, found beds and cleaned them, rewired stoves, sewn bed linen. We've used the trash from the street, brought it in from outside, re-formed it.

In the artists she passes, Jane sees newly established buds pushing their way through the hard earth. She sees a city reclaiming itself.

These people are turning New York into a work of art but it is not the kind of art that can be confined to a frame. Art comes from communities where the rent is cheap. If the rent is cheap, people can afford to live there. Artists have more time to spend on their art. The consequence of this is that their art improves, their art moves on, their art gets someplace. If they raze this neighbourhood to the ground this community will be destroyed and there will be no more art.

The city is not a work of art, thinks Jane. It is not an object. It is not static and still. It is not something to be admired from a distance – it is a process. It is a place for art to be created, but the borders of this island are not the borders of a painting.

Jane gathers together a great force that sweeps through neighbourhoods with a petition against the highway proposals. Men, women and children hand out fliers and talk directly to the public.

She tells reporters that the planners mustn't be allowed to build this highway. Building another highway isn't going to reduce congestion. It is senseless to encourage more people to drive. What we need is better public transportation. Invest in the city's buses and the subway. Tell people to leave their cars at home. Commissioner Moses belongs to another age. He does not understand the modern generation. Ask ordinary people what they want, and they'll tell you. They want a city that's easy to live in. They want their kids to be able to play safely in the street.

Robert Moses has built his headquarters beneath the Triborough Bridge on Randall's Island in the East River. This office is not the Gracie Mansion. This office is not Shangri-La. It has been built solely for utilitarian reasons. His office sits under the northern section of the bridge.

Automobiles run overhead. Further south, Moses has built sports facilities: baseball diamonds, a soccer field and tennis courts. Pathways have been laid for walking. Even Hell Gate to the east, through which the East River gushes at a pace, seems artificial, like nature is working in reverse, stripping everything back, the water not wet. One feels compressed by the Triborough Bridge. The bridge exists to move the traffic and the sports fields exist to move the people.

Robert Moses works in the stadium theatre at Jones Beach too. Here, he shows important guests how things are done in New York. They think, If this man can build this beach then he can build anything.

He tells them, I used to say to my engineers, I know you can build bridges, but can you build *beautiful* bridges?

They like to listen to his stories. They like to hear about important men.

I said to the President, you might be set to spread this money around the country but you won't find a better location for it than New York. Roosevelt is a man who knows when he's beaten. Oh, these politicians complain about me to the press but I'm the one they call when they want something done. I always say you can draw any kind of picture you like on a clean slate, but when you operate in an overbuilt metropolis, you have to hack your way with a meat axe. You can't make an omelette without breaking eggs.

He shows his guests to their seats. He can tell whether he's got them by the time the curtains separate. Moses doesn't stay to watch the performance. He retires to his office where he continues to work. A newspaper reporter once asked him what he thought of relaxation. Robert Moses said, You mean, besides a waste of time?

Tilted Arc is a twelve-feet-high steel wall that stands in the Federal Plaza. Because of its position in the plaza, a public space used by office workers going to and from work and taking lunch breaks, the arc has caused many problems. People are forced to navigate around it. The tilt of the arc causes a strong effect. It makes the arc seem like it is moving and this changes the nature of the person's perception of the surrounding space, not only through the interruption of movement but also because the arc appears to change shape as they move around it.

Some people say the arc attracts vandalism. It creates opportunities for crime. They say, *I don't want to walk around the other side of that wall only to see a gang waiting. I don't want to be mugged because of your art.*

We would just like to get from a to b without having to walk an extra one hundred and twenty feet around a piece of rusting steel.

Others say it is just like this city to give money away for idiotic projects like this, taking up public space with a hunk of filthy metal, when all people want to do is walk from this side of the plaza to that side without a problem on their lunch break.

But others say that this obstruction is exactly what we all need – that is the point, that is exactly what all good art should do – stop you in your tracks.

Eventually, the arc is removed.

The sudden space, the opening up of the plaza, is overwhelming to those who had grown used to the arc.

Some still walk the long way around, following old pathways. The secretaries who occupy the lower ground floor say they miss it. Yes, they can see out to the street now, but they say they liked the surprise.

28

I sense destruction, Bucke thinks. I sense an end coming. I sense that all things must end. I have written many endings. I have taken it upon myself to clarify how things must end.

Tell me about censorship, Bucke says.

I refused to give in, says Walt. I refused to take one line out. Each was integral to the overall sense. If I removed one I would be removing them all. If I removed one I would be removing limbs. I would be removing myself. Without the words I have chosen, there is nothing. If you deny me words, I cannot speak. If it is not written down, it did not happen. If a path is not laid, there is nowhere to go. If you don't remember, there is nothing to forget. It did not happen anyway. It is not over. You cannot just extract parts. Where the colour is, where the music is, where the bridge leads to, where the weather goes, what the tide is for, where the tops of buildings reach, where the rain lands, hitting us in the face, salt stains, tears and the ocean. Everything is connected, Bucke. They banned me in Boston because they said my work was explicit. But this was only because they didn't understand that all things are connected. Physical love is the same as the changing seasons. It is the same as the movement of the tide or the evolution of a city. By banning my work, they were dismissing all nature. All things in nature are good.

Bucke writes this down.

They are sitting in the grass a short distance from the train. Other passengers look stiff and awkward in their new surroundings. The flat land around them stretches further than is reasonable. It stretches one's insides and pulls at the mind. But here Walt can breathe. He lies down and moves his hands back and forth through the grass.

He remembers standing on the shoreline at Coney Island. The sand continued before him under the ocean. In his pocket he had slipped many pages ripped from books. He ripped the pages from books so that he wouldn't have to carry such a heavy weight. He had brought them to the edge of the land. But this was not the edge because the land continued under the water. He wanted to release the extracted pages and let the wind take them so that they could be freer than him. He plunged his hand into his pocket. He waited for something to happen but it did not. In his memory he waits there still. He is poised at the edge of the water.

This is like a photograph he has had taken in his Camden home. He sat in a chair beside the window while his friend Thomas Eakins positioned his camera. He told Walt to be still and so Walt fixed his eyes on a mark on the wall. Sometimes he thinks he is still waiting there, waiting for the picture to come to an end, which of course it never does, for he is always present in it. This is what he feels as he lies in the grass. The grass grows against him but one day it will grow through him.

The train whistle blows. Bucke stands. Walt does not get

up. Bucke walks towards the train. He catches the talk of other passengers as they walk. They are talking about New York. How excited they are to be going there. Do hurry, the woman behind him is saying. He looks over his shoulder for Walt.

The train is moving at a steady pace through the fields. The other passengers do not seem to notice this. They are settled into their own routines, kept busy on the train with the printed word, with books and newspapers. Everything is designed to mimic an ordinary day. Lives are performed without concentration. These passengers will continue on to their final destinations. They will alight and never re-board. This is not so easy for Richard Maurice Bucke. He is in a heightened state of emotion. He is too aware of his surroundings. The fixed points are Walt's answers to his questions. When Bucke asks a sensible question he does not always hear a sensible answer. Let me write it, Walt says. I know what you want to say. It is better to allow Walt to hold the pen.

Walt takes the pen and ink and he takes Bucke's pages. He hunches over the work and scores sentences out. He turns the page on its side and writes in the margins. He turns the paper over and writes additional scenes on the reverse. It is better to let him do it. He is Walt Whitman. He knows the story better than anyone. Bucke can only scratch the surface. Bucke knows how the brain works but the brain is not everything. There is also the heart.

When the time comes, Walt will step down from the

train onto the platform in New York. A porter will hand him his trunk and bag. Walt will smile and wave at Bucke. He will walk into the crowd and be lost. Bucke will lose sight of his friend. Bucke will travel on to Canada alone. Bucke will return to his family from whom he has been separated for too long. At home he will sit in his study and lay out the pages of Walt's biography, creased and worn from the journey. He will read back his own words and he will read Walt's writing in the margins. He will remember his friend. The book will describe him in part but not as a whole. Some things cannot be accurately described. Love is one of those things.

29

What happens during sex is a spiritual transformation. There are no outlines, borders, or gaps between subjects. Robert Mapplethorpe looks his lovers directly in the eye when he has sex. To have many lovers does not mean that he doesn't love them. The constancy is not with the other person but with himself. The feeling of love comes as quickly as a camera flash.

Robert's celebrity portfolio includes: Kathleen Turner, sultry, sexy. Grace Jones, naked, painted, wired. Philip Glass and Robert Wilson, synchronized, elegant. Donald Sutherland, smart, intense. Iggy Pop, wide-eyed, expectant. *Edmund White Horizontal*. He is passive, angelic, his eyes are wide and his mouth is closed. *Edmund White, full-face close up, screaming*, no date.

Robert used to visit Coney Island with his grandmother. He always ignored the beach and the fairground rides. He ran to the freak show instead. He could hear the bustle of the fairground outside, in the sun, by the beach, where other people were having fun, the rumble of running footsteps on the boardwalk. But here, body parts were on display, twisted and engorged, extra limbs, missing limbs, displayed on stage and in glass cabinets, in the dark. The freaks in this show were presented like art.

Fully Automated Nikon
(Object/Objection/Objectivity)

(1973)

LAURIE ANDERSON

Laurie Anderson is walking down a Manhattan street, attracting all the attention.

Hey, pretty lady – wanna ride with me?

Get that sweet ass over here.

Come gimme a kiss.

In her hand is a semi-automatic Nikon.

Take a seat on my lap, baby.

She holds up the camera and takes his picture.

What the fuck are you doing? Get the fuck out of my face!

It is as if she has pulled a gun on him.

Some men pose. Some find the photographic act an extension of her evident willingness to have sex – the camera is her organ and they are getting fucked. They hold out their arms, willing and eager. They flip her the bird, hold up a fist. She holds up her camera, proud and defiant. She is turning their abuse into art.

Say cheese! she says.

30

The tour guide waits by the gift-store door with a board in her hand that reads 'Hard Times'. Edmund is standing on the sidewalk.

There are a number of things I must insist on, says the guide. Please don't touch the historical artefacts. I will be passing items around for you to hold. Do not lean against the walls or sit down on the furniture. This tenement was built in 1863. Since that date to its closure in the 1930s the building has housed over seven thousand residents. The Hard Times tour you have selected today focuses specifically on the economic depression of the 1870s. As we explore the house you will learn more about the German immigrants of that period through the story of the Gumpertz family. Through their eyes, you will gain a better understanding of the conditions many working-class families faced in the Lower East Side in the late nineteenth century.

Stephen Crane would have known the people who lived here, Edmund thinks. They would have been ordinary people. He would have looked into the whites of their eyes and seen the truth there. Crane would have turned that truth into fiction.

Please save any questions you have until later, the guide says. Please let me know if you get too hot. Please respect the rules of this house. Please respect the memories of the dead.

The memories of the dead. But they are everywhere, Edmund thinks.

Now please follow me.

Edmund and the other tourists cram themselves into the dark and narrow corridor. The wallpaper is hanging off the walls and a single dangling light bulb glares bare above.

Now it's very dark in here, says the guide. And the wallpaper, as you can see, is black. The discoloration of the walls is due to the poor conditions in which these people lived. None of these tenements had ventilation and everybody cooked on coal-powered stoves. Now turn around and look at the paintings on the wall.

The painting behind Edmund is dirty. He can't see what the picture is. The painting on the opposite wall shows a rural scene. A cornfield, trees, bright blue sky.

This scene was painted to remind the immigrants of where they had come from, says the guide. They wouldn't have been able to see the painting, however, on account of all the smoke. Would someone please switch off the light?

Darkness.

The only light in this hallway would have been one oil lamp placed in that window. Can you imagine living mostly in the dark? Now follow me.

The tenement upstairs is divided into three separate rooms. There is a bedroom, a kitchen and a parlour. Electric fans nudge warm air. A dishrag hangs on the corner of the stove. There is a cutting board with a knife and a slice of bread. Unlaced boots stand in the corner of the room. The bed is made. The eiderdown is neatly tucked. An oil lamp burns in the corner of the room. It is difficult to breathe in here. The other visitors look uncomfortable. They stand with their backs against the wall. They stand with arms folded, hands interlaced. They are looking directly at the floor. This apartment is not like theirs. They are standing in a stranger's house. The guide passes Edmund a heavy clothes iron. Edmund holds it in the palm of his hand.

The mother kept it hot on the stove, says the guide. Mrs Gumpertz scrubbed the floors to prevent disease.

Mrs Gumpertz had memories of a home back in Germany, thinks Edmund. She remembered the colour and the smell of her village. She had come to New York for a better life. She thought about the lives of her children. Everything she did was for the sake of their future. She suffered great hardship – the death of a child, abandonment by her husband – yet she and her daughters survived.

Mrs Gumpertz became a dressmaker and she sewed fine clothes for New York's upper classes, the guide says. Her work must have been greatly admired, for she earned enough money to support herself and her children. Inspectors came to ensure her living quarters were clean because disease was regularly passed from the slums to higher society through workers in the textiles trade.

Mrs Gumpertz was a fastidious cleaner. A filthy city does not necessarily mean a filthy home. Edmund leans against the wall. He feels the hard impressions of the wallpaper against his back. His sweat is soaking through his shirt. The dirt on the wall will now mark his clothes.

The guide is holding up a photograph of two blonde girls in present time. They are twins, eight or nine years old. They are standing in the sunshine in a garden beside a swimming pool. They are wearing Mickey Mouse T-shirts and holding tennis rackets. The guide says these are the descendants of Mrs Gumpertz.

It is their history we are witnessing today, says the guide. There is always another story to tell. This is what we want to show you at the Tenement Museum. We want to forge a link between the past and the present. The history we describe always comes from real individuals. We never describe fictional people. The Gumpertz family really lived here once.

The girls are smiling in the photograph. Their teeth are very white. They are rich and healthy-looking. They look like girls who don't know about history.

The visitors file out of the tenement. Edmund waits in empty space for a moment longer. He crosses the kitchen to the bedroom and looks at the empty bed there.

The next tenement is empty of items except for debris piled on the floor, masonry, floorboards, kitchen cabinets. The wallpaper is falling away from the wall. Stacks of beams are piled in the corner. Exposed electrical wire is hanging from the ceiling. There is no furniture, no family portraits here. There are no personal items, no clothes, no dolls.

This building closed in the 1930s, says the guide. The

landlord couldn't afford to maintain it during the economic hardships of the Depression. The building stood empty for fifty years until the 1980s when the founders of the Tenement Museum discovered it. Our director couldn't believe what she had found. One day she was walking through the Lower East Side. She stopped at the store downstairs to use the bathroom. What she saw inside was a time capsule. Every room was exactly as it had been left. The landlord had repaired holes in the walls by shoving newspaper into them and papering over the holes. When we moved in we found twenty layers of wallpaper in some of the rooms. We found one hundred and fifty years of journalism stuffed into those walls. Many of the problems the city has today are the same as they were in Mrs Gumpertz's day. Housing is still a major problem. Many people can't afford to live in this neighbourhood now. This problem is spreading through the city.

The group files down the fire escape. Edmund sees the glass towers ascending high above the horizon. Cranes are swinging steel beams into place. He remembers a photographic portrait he once had taken. In it, he was screaming. Edmund couldn't look at it, this silent screaming man. Had he known from the beginning to think of his life as an ongoing narrative instead of as an accumulation of individual moments, he might have foreseen the bigger picture and thus protected his heart. They called him a pioneer. He doesn't know what he has discovered except a broken heart.

—

Outside the Chelsea Hotel on West 23rd Street, the guide says to the group:

When the Chelsea opened in 1884, it contained luxury apartments. As the entertainment industry spread uptown, however, after the completion of the subway's first line in 1904, rich residents vacated and moved uptown too. The apartments in this building were segmented and made smaller. The owners advertised for residents from the lower middle classes. During the Depression the apartments were again made smaller. This was when the artists came.

Edmund thinks, They stayed in luxury suites that had been cut up and reordered. They lived in rooms with half a fireplace, half a ceiling rose. The outlines of the rooms were brand new and their borders were confusing. Ghost apartments. Ghost hotel. Artists made use of smaller quarters. They didn't care about the size. It was the low rent that mattered and the company. The sign on the door reads *Renovation In Progress*. The windows of the hotel have been boarded up. Every room must now stand empty. The hotel's residents have moved on. When the renovation is complete, it will be a tourist hotel. Visitors will come to choose their rooms from a menu. The beds will be made with clean white sheets. There will be a concierge. A neat clerk will sit behind a bare desk. This building will not now produce anything new. It will live off the memories of previous times. What Edmund is looking at is memory only. This memory is not one of his. It is the memory of a city that is always changing. Visitors will choose rooms that best reflect their characters. Will they imagine for a moment that they are Patti Smith? Will they come here for a holiday from themselves?

Fifth Avenue has been cordoned off and crowds are gathering. Music and drums echo off the buildings. Floats creep past. Dancers are dressed as superheroes. Batman shakes his ass and spanks Robin. A marching band with baton-twirlers. The musicians are young men wearing evening gowns. There are Medusas and Evita Peróns, Marilyn Monroes and a female Elvis. Mothers and fathers hold up banners that read 'I love my gay son'. Men dance with men. Women dance with women. A convertible with the top down drives slowly past, princess-men sitting in the back waving like the Queen of England; their make-up has smudged. Boys and girls hand out cups of water and towels. The paraders pat themselves dry and smile for the cameras. The music changes from marching bands to drum and bass, from jazz to honky-tonk piano. A woman with a shaved head plays a classical piano on the back of a yellow pick-up truck. A DJ balances on a float, one hand stuck to a set of pink headphones. She dances. Transvestite Miss Americas in sequined evening gowns wave stiffly from the back of a blue van. Banners read, *Whole Foods support gay marriage*; *Gay Marriage = Gay Registry = Gay Clutter. Store with us!*

But Edmund remembers love.

31

A reporter watches a promotional film from 1949 that shows the high towers of Stuyvesant Town, an eighty-acre high-rise development in the Lower East Side that was built at the suggestion of Robert Moses. The film shows dozens of housing blocks built in landscaped gardens. Families are sitting on the grass with their children. Couples are strolling slowly along the pathways. Old people are sitting on benches and feeding the birds.

The narration describes the miracle born to this area, once the site of slums and depravity – abandoned gas works and run-down tenements – people now have somewhere clean to live, modern apartments with grass, children's play areas, and a perimeter fence.

The voice-over says,

What was once a run-down, dying section of the great city of New York has been recreated and today this section is a beautiful park-like community. Yesterday there was hardly a patch of green to be found anywhere in this district. Today there are many acres of lawns and shady trees and miles of winding walks close to everybody's apartment. Yesterday, children had to play on the sidewalks or fire escapes or in the dangerous streets but today there are safe play facilities for boys and girls of all ages.

The film doesn't mention those who lived in the Gas

House District who have been evicted from their homes or the fact that the people living in the development now are all middle class, married and white.

The reporter reads back his notes for what Moses said about this.

It is well within the rights of the board to accept who they want into the estate. To let just anybody in would lower the value of the property and be detrimental to their annual yield.

Also:

What do I believe? I believe in limited objectives and in getting things done. If you want a text, let me quote George Bernard Shaw from the dedication of Man and Superman. *'This', says Shaw, 'is the true joy in life, the being used for a purpose recognized by yourself as a mighty one; the being thoroughly worn out before you are thrown on the scrap heap; the being the force of Nature instead of a feverish, selfish little clod of grievances complaining that the world will not devote itself to making you happy.' Those were the words of a courageous man and I can add nothing to them.*

Rimbaud in New York
(1978–79)
DAVID WOJNAROWICZ

The photograph depicts a man wearing a mask, the face of Arthur Rimbaud, that look he has, slightly askance, ready for anything.

Arthur Rimbaud is staring at you through the crowds that pass the 25-cent peep shows of 42nd Street.

Arthur Rimbaud is lying on a bed, looking up at you. He is masturbating.

Arthur Rimbaud is taking a leak in a toilet. His piss arches clear before a smutty wall.

Arthur Rimbaud lies on a bed. A man is nuzzling his naked chest.

Arthur Rimbaud stands on a beach, the tide and a trail of rocks stretching behind him. A sailing boat is passing along the horizon.

Arthur Rimbaud slumps against a wall. Behind him is a target. A needle is sticking out of his arm.

———

Arthur Rimbaud is sitting on the subway, surrounded by people and graffiti. No one is looking at him.

David Wojnarowicz looks at the camera. His mouth is all sewn up.

32

The tide is turning for Robert Moses. The public of 1965 are angry. On whose authority does he knock these neigh-bourhoods down? What right does he have to build a road or a bridge? He is not an elected official, yet he is allowed to do this? He is pushing out the poor and inviting traffic in. The streets are clogged with vehicles, and the more roads he builds, the worse it gets. He says to people, If you don't like it then move out. He says, Find another place to live. He calls working-class districts 'slums' but these places are where ordinary people live. Without ordinary people this city would be nothing. Who built this city to begin with? The labourers and manufacturers, the shopkeepers and traders. They have always lived in the city. Old tene-ments must be refurbished and rent-controlled. You cannot eradicate problems by bulldozing the past.

The public unite and take to the streets. They talk to the press. Journalists research cover stories and interview resi-dents. They take photographs. They investigate claims of corruption. Television crews come to record the action. There are public meetings and demonstrations. Finally, things are beginning to change.

33

In Times Square there's an M&M's World, a Disney Store and a Bubba Gump Shrimp restaurant. There's a Wendy's and a Hard Rock Café and a McDonald's and a TGI Fridays. Edmund strolls into the Times Square Visitor Center. This used to be a theatre once. Now, it contains information and historical artefacts. Photographs and memorabilia of Times Square line the walls. Where rows of seats once stood in the centre of the room there is now just space. On the stage a cinema screen is showing a documentary film about New York's past. These are eras Edmund can remember.

He remembers the look-back, the walk-up, the exchange of money for sex. He remembers the boys coming in from the country looking for a quick buck and a place to stay for the night, and the men who were only too happy to help. He remembers the dark movie houses and the cinema screens hanging over theatre stages. The real-life actors were replaced by movies, depictions of people fucking on a screen. The acting was bad but the scenes were explicit and that's what you had come here to see – bodies penetrating other bodies. He remembers the live acts that were brought in to warm up the show. A man and woman would enter and do their business on the stage for all to see. It was lacklustre and mechanical. The audience clapped politely when the man finally came on the woman's backside. He remembers the trash and the dirt outside the theatres, the hanging on the street, knowing everybody by different names. He remembers how good it was. Every time, he met someone new. Every time, he was a different Edmund White.

Here is the original storefront for the Peep-O-Rama and an example of the viewing booth – put a quarter in the slot and watch the fairground ride. All Edmund sees are time restrictions and imitative art. He sees the inconvenience and the disappointment that comes from watching images shown in a booth, how the imagination cannot replace what should really be there – the touch of a real body or the smell of the streets. He remembers ordering the men who were imperfect. And so the city was the same, that filthy place, which didn't work. What is it now? A historical exhibition of a cleaned-out place.

34

The residents of East Tremont in the Bronx are going about their daily business in 1950. Pedestrians can barely move down the teeming sidewalks for they are filled with people coming in and out of the tenements, entering and exiting the stores. The tenement blocks are full. People are hanging out of windows, watching the passing day. The grocery stores and butcher shops are thriving. The tailors and delis are full. The roads are jammed with trucks, cars and wagons. Everybody knows everybody here. You can't walk ten yards without knocking into someone you know. This person is a second cousin of this person. This person is related to you by marriage. You grew up with this fellow, sat next to him in school, lived in the apartment above that one. People are watching the street through windows, from stoops, store doorways, barber chairs, bar stools, grocery stoops. Kids are playing in the streets. They play stickball, jump rope, play for penny games, tag, pram pushing, kicking cans, baseball. The kids are ragged and loud. A woman in a third-floor apartment yells down to the kids on the street. The weather is unseasonably hot. The women bring out chairs onto the street and they sit down, cross one foot over the other and lean back. These moments. Stillness in the busy street. Women return home with groceries. Now there are other jobs to do. It is all right; the kids are being watched by the neighbours. The kids play in the alleyways and under the storefront awnings, in the shade, swipe an apple or two from the grocer and run. When the men return from work in the evening they sit out on the stoops.

One day in December in 1952, 1,530 households along a one-mile stretch of East Tremont receive a letter from Commissioner Moses telling them they have ninety days to move.

Ninety days?

What is this? What is this you're telling me?

They want us to move?

Move where?

What money do we have for this?

I was born here. So were my children.

Ninety days?

I'm not going anywhere.

You must be joking.

Move from this place? No way in hell.

The residents form a neighbourhood alliance. They protest. They petition the mayor. They gain the support of the mayor and the elected borough officials. The residents are told not to worry. This issue will be cleared up soon. It will be sorted out. Don't worry about it. Just go on with your ordinary lives, they say.

But they don't know Robert Moses.

The residents are eventually shipped out. Generations of families, neighbours, businesses. 1,530 households are packed up, moved on. In come the engineers, the construction workers, and the bulldozers. The buildings are razed. The land is cleared.

Robert Moses and his army watch the protestors light a bonfire in the street. One of the men points to a figure being hoisted high and thrown into the flames.

Hey, Bob, is that you?

The figure is ablaze.

Why, so it is, says Moses. Quite a likeness, he laughs.

How The Other Half Lives
(1890)
JACOB RIIS

A mother, father and five children are sitting in one room of a tenement, a single bed to one side of the room and a cot in the centre. The father is perched on a wooden crate and holding onto the cot. The flash has rendered the family pale, their skin white and glaring, blank. Coats, clothes are hung up in the back room, every shelf stuffed with pots and pans and equipment, the floor swept but not clean.

Seven men are crammed into a tenement room, two men resting upon a dirty mattress, raised upon a mezzanine. One man is sitting up and leaning forward, the other lying flat on his back. Both pairs of feet are bare and dirty. Boots and socks stand upon the floor before three other men trying to sleep covered over with blankets and sheets. The rest of the room is filled with trunks and boxes. The camera flash reveals the dirty marks on the walls and ceiling.

One boy is riding on the back of another in a playground. The children in the background are climbing up and down ladders that are secured over a single climbing beam. Beyond the playground is a tenement building. Some of the curtain blinds are drawn, some are open. The boy hanging on the older boy's back is looking at the camera.

A crowd is huddling on the street in winter before a burnt-out tenement building that is covered with ice. A hose lies on the ground in front of them. Some of the icicles hanging from the ledges of glassless windows are feet-long. From the viewpoint of a dark alleyway, the building, covered as it is in ice, is white and bright, cleaner than the crowd standing on the sidewalk, brighter than the filthy alley walls.

35

I have told you about the photographs I have had taken, how Eakins has captured my image and how I remain there still on paper. Mathew Brady also took my photograph. He photographed many other important men. He took photographs of soldiers in the war, those who were living and those who were dead. He photographed the battlefields. He wants people to be able to see history with their own eyes rather than rely on the subjective words of others. He wants his photographs to create an accurate history. His photographs mean these men will never be forgotten.

I have my own memories of this time. I don't know if they are as reliable. When I went to look for my brother the men did not look me in the eye and I was glad of it. I picked a path through them. I asked a nurse where my brother was. Brother? she said. Darkness was falling. I listened to the men as they moaned. I could not write about this stubby hill, this nightfall. I could not move. Lucky are we who live so internally – the guns can never get us, I thought. I had possibly lost a brother. The rest of the men will fall like dominoes. At the surgeon's tent I found the doctor. His face was as grey as the bed sheets. Do you know where my brother is? I asked. There he was on the bed in the corner of the tent. George was not dead. George was alive and lying in the bed. He was not so greatly changed. There was only a scar on his cheek that would heal very soon. I felt at the time we had been saved. I realize now that death had only been delayed for it will come to us all in time.

The tents lined up for nearly a mile – the battle had not gone well – you could see it in the faces of the dying men and in the bloody limbs scattered across the ground, in the tears in the flesh, white fat, blue veins, blue skin, fingers and arms. The outcome could be read in the flesh. The limbs at the top of the piles were fresh and pink. Some feet retained boots, too rotten to remove, though the rings had been pulled from all the fingers. I watched the soldiers sleeping. I watched death take them. Often, there were things they wanted to be known before they died. They asked me to write their letters. I resisted the urge to add flourishes of phrasing, even though the letters would have been greatly improved by this. I wanted their letters to be authentic. When the writing was done I read the letters back and felt satisfied to read someone else's words written in my own hand. But war is not something you can describe, Bucke. You cannot do it with words or images. When we look back at something, we look back as if through a gauze. The only truth is that of the present moment.

36

It starts as a way to get good at something. Lisa Lyon goes for the weights the other women don't look at. Everyone watches when she lifts those bells, her hands and her arms held high in the air. She is breathtaking. On the beach, in the sun, she wears a bikini. The definition of her muscle punctuates her body, which is not mammoth, though it is very large and strong, and dazzling in the sunlight as she lifts the bells.

Lisa is more interesting than the male bodybuilders because she is something unexpected. She makes people look twice, once at her body, and once again, looking for the reason why. They never find the answer. They never get past the body.

The way she sees it is that, if you're talking about some kind of animal, a cat, a wild cat, a lion, for example, if you're talking about a lion and you see the lion running across the plain as it chases the antelope, you don't say, look at that female lion or look at that male lion, you say, look at that animal. Lisa says there should be no gender distinctions. We should exist only in terms of physical form.

When Robert Mapplethorpe sees Lisa for the first time, he

cannot get over the way she looks. He says to a friend it's a shame about the scar on her face. She would have been perfect if it wasn't for the scar.

What scar? the friend says.

When she comes out of the bathroom, Robert sees that she has no scar at all. The black mark on her face was just ash from her cigarette. When they meet they laugh about this.

In the chill of the city, Lisa scurries over to Robert's studio in the heavy coat Robert bought for her and the jewellery she spent her savings on – crashing against her chest as she walks, slamming into muscle. Covered up like this, she feels unusual, but once she gets out of the cold and into his studio, she reveals herself like a superhero. She holds herself perfectly still, her biceps flexed and taut, one leg straight, the other bent, her arm in the air, just one arm, just one bicep, the angular line of her buttocks, the square jaw, the tiny nose, small eyes, solid stomach, fully-formed thighs. Robert, his assistant and the woman who sorts his bills stand there looking at her. There are no more photographs yet she continues to flex.

Robert sees in Lisa the same thing she sees. They are both interested in form. Together, they come up with a plan. Lisa is dressed up in all the things she can be: natural and made up, as a hero and a victim, in high heels and stockings, in all the things that are sexy: as Eve, as a bride, as a man. They get carried away. They are like children. They go everywhere together. She is a good replacement for Patti, but she does not want to possess him. She is all the male parts he isn't and he's all the slyness and the cunning she is not. Together they form one whole person. It is not like it is with Patti Smith, who is all art and intellect. No, this is about bodies and form. Lisa looks at the photographs, all the women she can be. But she is always Lisa.

They make a book together. It is called *Lady, Lisa Lyon*. They drive out to the desert, just Lisa and Robert. As they are passing through small-town America she looks over at Robert who has fallen asleep against the glass. His hair is long and curly. He is like her beautiful girlfriend. She strokes the side of his face. She catches her arm in the rearview mirror and is taken off-guard by the ripple of muscle. This is the body she knows better than any other yet it still takes her by surprise.

Lisa stands on the desert rock. It is already midday. The sun is scorching. Robert is distracted. Robert is getting it all wrong. She can tell by the way he is frowning and getting her to do the same poses over and over. She doesn't tell him that the angle of light is incorrect. Oh no, she doesn't say a thing.

Lying in the motel room Lisa listens to Robert throwing up in the bathroom. He is ill. But they are here, the two of them, in this motel, so far away from New York.

Can I get you anything? she calls out. Don't you want something to eat?

He stumbles out. He switches off all the lights. The smell of vomit wafts over her. He goes to the window and looks out. In the orange light he looks so young. He doesn't seem to know where he is.

What are you looking at? she says.

He blinks.

She holds out her hand. He lies down next to her. She pulls him in. His skinny body is cold and clammy against her sunburnt chest. She rubs him better. He snaps awake like someone has flicked a switch, and then they are fucking.

As a child, Lisa had nightmares. As she grew up she used the physical pursuit of excellence to help her sleep at night. Sometimes she writes poetry. Other times she dances.

Robert, are you coming to bed?

But he is in the bathroom and he doesn't want to come out. She wants to say to him that the longer he leaves it the worse it will be, putting off sleep, putting off dreaming, but he doesn't like to sleep. When he does, he sleeps all day, the lamplight in his studio is his own private moon.

They have sex in a motel room. The cheap, fascinating glow of the neon sign makes Lisa think of microwave ovens, extraterrestrial life, California. What sex always does – confuses reality with fiction. She holds him in her strong arms. He is so cold but she is warm because of the desert sun –

she thinks, we are like sleeping lions in Africa and nothing can hurt us.

In the studio Robert positions the lights so that they focus on the centre of Lisa's torso. She rolls her shoulders forward and tenses the muscles in her shoulders and her chest. She clasps her hands together. She holds the tension. She holds her face still. She pouts for him. It is all about the contrast between the beauty of her face and the strength of her body. It is all about how both of these things are the same. She holds it there, all of herself, in this position, and lets him take his picture.

Lisa and Robert go out together all the time. They have such fun. They are the same person. She doesn't mind the way he shows her off. She doesn't mind flexing her muscles for strangers.

Lisa frets about the pictures. She worries what they will show. She worries what Robert will see in them. Lisa looks at the photographs. They are very beautiful but this is not the life she hoped to see – it is a life she already knows, frozen in a frame. She sees form and she sees structure but nothing of what is inside. The shot of her body with the muscles pulled taut has been cropped at the neck. Robert says he will name her in the title but there will be no face. We do not need to see your face, he says. It's all about the body.

———

Painted head to toe in thick gold paint, Lisa lunges forward and back in the dark room, the beat of the music, tribal, bestial. There is only the body and the beat of the drum. This could be the beat of her heart. Electric, golden.

Robert poses Lisa with a python, a tiger and a scorpion. The animals he chooses are always exotic creatures and never ones she wants to hold. Lisa dresses in a catsuit and high-heeled boots, and holds an epileptic tiger by a leash. The point of this is to show the many sides of Lisa Lyon. She thinks about the tiger having fits, the chemical imbalance in its brain. Her body will be beautifully preserved in art, hung in galleries, bought at great expense. The tiger fits and shudders.

Lisa arrives for the launch of *Lady, Lisa Lyon*. The pictures and the books are on display. Lisa is wearing an elegant dress. Robert introduces her to influential people then leaves her so he can talk to other people. She sees the photographs. She cannot miss them. Journalists are asking her questions. She gives the usual answers: 5´3½, 105 lbs, May 13, 1953, French and Spanish, Best Deadlift: 225 lbs, Benchpress: 120 lbs, Squat: 265 lbs, Chest: 37˝, Waist: 22˝, Hips: 32˝. They ask about Robert. They ask about Patti.

After Robert gets sick, there are many interviews. They want to know if Lisa has been tested. They want to know what she makes of Robert's lifestyle. The steady stream of interviews and answering the same questions is an eternal performance. She wants to say – I'm in a book – it's that simple – you take me out of life and put me in the pages of a book, but it's him you want to know about. She shows them the book. She turns the pages for them. They ask if she's been tested. They ask if she'd like to comment. But don't you see what this means? They stare at her blankly. They write in their notebooks. They ask if she's lost any weight. They ask if she still trains. They ask if she has ever taken steroids. They ask if she's ever been tested – you slept with him, right? They ask if Robert has taken steroids. They want to know everything. She has nothing to say.

After Robert dies, they stop asking questions.

37

The High Line is an elevated platform along which steam trains used to transport industrial goods up and down the west side of Manhattan. Edmund has read that before then a cowboy used to ride in front of the train to warn pedestrians of its approach. Edmund has known his fair share of cowboys along this railway line, beneath the elevated track, in the shadows, in the dark.

Edmund walks along the High Line, tripping on the railway tracks that lie embedded in the path. The flowers in the flowerbeds are the same species as those that grew wild during the years the track stood abandoned between the 1980s and 2009. Crowds of people have come to see the High Line. They walk in packs, covering the walkway, stopping to touch and smell the flowers in the borders, removing shoes and walking on the grass, stopping to pose before the view of the Empire State Building, leaning against the rail with a hip dropped and a fixed smile, then exchanging with a friend, passing the camera over to allow the other person to pose, back and forth, different views, the same views. They stop in the middle of the path to take their photographs. They photograph Tenth Avenue below them, the bright cobbled streets of the Meatpacking District.

There is a similar park in Paris. It runs along an elevated

line. Edmund liked to walk there when it was raining. Edmund walked alone through the Promenade Plantée and he thought of the shadows beneath the western elevated track in New York. He thought about what he did in the past.

In those days he dressed understated – jeans, T-shirt, sneakers never shoes. It was not the thing to look smart and polished. You had to look natural, available, desirable. He used to go out very late at night. He stood on the corner of Gansevoort and Washington Street, pausing on the cobblestones turned bright by the moon. The elevated track loomed behind him. He imagined the old market stalls beneath, the exchange of dollars for meat, remnants still visible, the reek of flesh, noise, cacophony, butchers' stores now turned over to other uses. He followed a group of men through a doorway. He descended the steep flight of stairs. The booming bass of the club filled his body. He felt he was part of the mass. They were all in this together, he thought. He was standing in an expansive underground space. Everybody was dancing with him. There was music, laughter and conversation. He was very grateful for the noise. Time spilled over into the nextnextnext. He couldn't separate the bodies from one another or from the beat until the music stopped and they all shuffled wearily to the door. This guy who had his hand on him stepped away and the club was quiet. The men filed slowly up the stairs. Light hit Edmund like the silence, the dawn having broken, market traders and retailers setting up for the day.

A new outpost of the Whitney Museum of Art is being

built beside the High Line. Edmund reads the sign – *The Whitney is an idea, not a building.*

New apartment buildings stand along the park's edge. As Edmund walks he looks into the empty rooms. He sees sleek grey furniture: a couch, a table, a solitary chair. The balconies are swept very clean. The view of the residents will be the long line of a railway, but instead of the rattle and boom of industrial shipments the residents will hear the chatter and laughter of tourists who walk up and down the path in the sun. They will see them sitting out on wooden deck chairs, on lunch breaks, on holiday, taking photographs.

The Empire State Building stands to his right. He sees the Chelsea Piers to his left. Rainbow flags and advertisements for storage space are stuck onto the sides of the buildings. Ahead of him is a viewing platform where there are rows of benches and a glass wall through which he sees traffic flowing up Tenth Avenue. Here is the Meatpacking District, its industrial structures, the narrow cobbled streets he used to know. Children are pressing their hands against the glass of the viewing platform and looking down. Men, women and children are sitting at restaurant tables on the sidewalks, eating sandwiches.

38

The reporter rushes into his editor's office.

Get up to the Bronx and take a look around, the editor says. They're knocking down the last tenement any day now but some old guy's refusing to get out.

The reporter climbs the stairs to the fifth floor. He is watchful of the spaces where the wood has rotted. The man is waiting for him at the top of the stairs. The man recognizes the extent of the climb with a nod. The reporter follows him into the apartment. He tests the floorboards with his foot as he goes. He steps over the objects on the floor – radiator, bathtub, oil drum. He scrapes his ankle against something sharp and curses.

How long do you plan on living here? the reporter asks.

The walls are black with dirt.

Look. Nothing sticks any more, the man says.

The man lifts up a piece of sodden wallpaper hanging from the wall.

In the room there is a mattress and a heap of dirty clothes. A gas burner and lamp are positioned on a broken chair.

The man sits down on the bed. The reporter knows this man can't win. This fight was over before it began. This man cannot beat Robert Moses. He cannot beat that formidable man.

The reporter goes into the bathroom and closes the door. He runs water into the basin. He splashes water onto his face and turns off the faucet. He dries his face with the sleeve of his coat and holds his sleeve to his nose to breathe in the cologne. He looks at himself in the mirror. It isn't his own face he sees reflected back. It is another man's face he sees in the wall. Another man is standing in the neighbouring apartment, looking at him through a hole in the wall where the mirror should be. This man does not flinch. This man does not shout. This man does not even seem to notice. This man stares at the reporter as if it is his own face he sees reflected back. The man smooths back his hair, looks left, looks right.

CENTRAL PARK, 1956

The engineers in Central Park decide that they must go for lunch. In their hurry to get out of the sun, they leave behind the plans for the new parking lot. A young mother who has been playing with her son in the adjacent playground collects up the billowing sheets of paper. The plans show the outline of a marked perimeter extending from the existing parking lot into the park, encircling the nearby trees, the flower borders, the shrubs.

When the woman gets home she calls her friend.

They're destroying the park! she cries.

I'll be right over!

This isn't just any neighbourhood; this is the Upper West Side.

Within half an hour the troops are rallied. Residents have made banners and boards displaying their hatred for Parks Commissioner Robert Moses.

Reporters follow like dogs behind. They interview the kids.

One father says, Our children might as well be playing in the street if this goes through.

Parents tell their children to make a racket. Look what they're doing to your park! The children are excited and some are screaming, crying because they don't like the drama. This means the papers get their shots.

When the press interview Robert Moses he says, I don't want to give the impression of being impatient but I don't have the time to argue about taking down a tree for a parking space.

Engineers are ordered to return to the park to cordon off the tree and cut it down. The protestors, holding hands, encircle the tree and they don't let go. The workmen are laughing because they're getting paid regardless and, anyways, they'll just come back tonight when the women are all tucked up in bed, which is what they do.

At the break of dawn, the children are dragged from their beds. Hey kid, don't you have some kind of war-playing kit, a uniform and a hand grenade? Great! Put it on! Get wailing! We're all in this together!

The children are dragged along the street, dragged out of sleep and out of dreaming. They arrive just in time to see the show. The men are hacking away at the tree.

A young boy watches. He trembles with excitement as the tree falls.

39

The reporter is waiting on the central lawn beside a high-rise block. There is a chill in the air, an early fall. He buttons his coat and looks out at the road.

A car pulls up. A city official gets out.

He walks towards the reporter and nods a greeting. They walk together across the lawn.

As you can see, the official says, we've gone a long way to ensure an attractive environment. The previous accommodation had no gardens. Residents used to have to walk fourteen blocks to get to the closest green space. Now it's right on their doorstep.

The grass is growing. Thick, waxy grass. Hard. A small area in the corner of the plot has been cordoned off and positioned. There is playground equipment, a slide, swings, but not many.

How many children will that serve? the reporter asks.

The numbers haven't been finalized yet. As I was saying, these people had no parks at all before.

The official points out the service exits and fire-escape provisions. The doorframes are freshly painted and the paths have been laid. Sturdy shrubs have been planted in the borders. Border railings have been secured.

And so the residents who are waiting to be relocated here, where are they living now? asks the reporter.

Temporary accommodation.
Which is where, exactly?

40

They are passing through farmland, past small home-steads, through cornfields. Walt sees the people who must have helped to build the railway living close to the line. Chimneys expel smoke. Washing lines nod in the breeze. Children are playing in the earth. Walt sees horses tied to posts. There is no station platform for these people. Workers rarely benefit from their own labour.

He takes *Leaves of Grass* from his trunk. He examines the cover and the spine. He begins to read 'Song of Myself' as Bucke has requested. It is a fine work and he likes to read it.

Bucke feels pinned to the wall. The woodland through which they are passing is dark. No light penetrates. Out the other side. Green fields. Farmland. Shacks. All goes unnoticed when Walt is reading.

In his notebook is a list of all the things people have said about Walt: it is an honour, pleasure and privilege to know him; we are filled with love, anxiety, awe; he is a rogue, a beast and a scoundrel, incomparable, inconceivable, insurmountable.

And a description from a veteran, who, when Bucke asked what he remembered of the war, said this:

They wanted to take my leg on account of the infection.

But I didn't want it to be taken. I was mad. The fear was worse than the pain. I didn't know what to do. I explained myself to a nurse. I told him I wanted to keep my leg. I pleaded with him to do something, but he didn't need to be persuaded. He went directly to the doctor and demanded they leave my leg alone. They did. I recovered. I owe this man my life. He helped me to recover. He fed me. He supported my head when I needed to drink. He sat so close to me on the bed that I could feel the warmth of his body through the blanket. He had such kind eyes. I have never seen such a face before. I remember him perfectly. I still dream about him.

Was the man's name Walt Whitman? Bucke asked.

The soldier's face lit up like the dawn.

Will you be happy to get to New York? Walt says.

Bucke cannot answer. He looks out the window at the passing land. The sky has grown dark.

The Ballad of Sexual Dependency
(1986)

NAN GOLDIN

Nan Goldin turns off all the lights, downs her drink and looks beyond her audience at the air vent on the back wall of the bar. She imagines her narration coming directly out from the photographs she is displaying on the screen, shooting out over these people's heads, through the vent and onto the streets of New York. Nan begins and ends in this room in the Bowery, but after tonight traces of her will be found all over the city. The audience will look at their hands and see traces of Nan's blood. They will look in the mirror and see in their faces traces of Nan's love, or they will see the colour blue, which is the colour of the bathroom in which she took the photograph of herself reflected in a mirror, where the sun caught her face, or they will see the rooftops of Manhattan and the man, so arrogant, the one who battered her, sitting against the wall on the roof with the whole of New York City behind him, sitting there with his shoe untied, completely in command of his own face and her attitude, Nan's bruised face, now an object of art.

These photographs are just a hint of how beautiful everything is.

If the man who battered her dreamt at all, it was a dog dream, with fleas and hunger and a picture-perfect link between what he had done and the pictures she took of her face the next day, of the thing she saw there in her face when she looked in the mirror and held up the camera, when she could barely see because the bruise on her face was as inflamed as a badly pummelled peach.

The photographs she displays on the screen are not moments from her past, they are moments extracted from it. The images begin and end within the frame of the shot, and the world is contained there.

She dedicates the sequence to her sister, who showed great courage one day in lying down on the commuter tracks in Washington DC and waiting for the train.

The last image flickers on the screen and she turns off the projector. The audience applauds and she walks off-stage. She gets a drink at the bar like an ordinary person. She remains in the same place, as a seed does, burrowed down, showing excellent potential, buried in a basement bar in New York City. Her camera is stored safely behind the bar with a virgin roll of film.

Her art is related to the death of her sister but Nan refuses to let this become the focus. She thinks of the batterer's face and wonders whether showing a photograph of him isn't just the same fucking thing as showing a picture of a train.

The ability to love is a rare gift. Nan shows it through the photographs she takes, but the photographs also show how she possesses people.

After her sister's death, Nan had an affair with an older man and learnt what it meant to be truly sexual. This man took advantage of her body and of her grief, and she wanted him to. She wanted to be whole by connecting with another. She wanted to live every moment to its fullest in case it was her last. She wanted her sister to see that what had happened didn't matter. All the while she thought of her sister. It was like she was giving life to her by fucking him. She transformed this man into her father then she transformed herself into her sister, and the train and the tunnel and this nation's capital all formed a link, and she was the apex of that link, the connecting part, the coupling, the coupler between the engine and the carriages behind. She lingered there in the arms of a stranger. She felt young and alive. She felt unconscious like her sister. She felt limbless.

She photographed every part of her body. She recorded every part of her life in vivid colour. She wanted to be that woman in the photograph. She wanted suddenness. She wanted to see the detail. She wanted to blow her own mind with the detail. She wanted the blood to be a deep red, like a certain shade of lipstick, like the colour of her bloodshot eye after she was battered. She wanted someone to find beauty in that comparison.

Nothing is real.

What is real to Nan is this hot basement bar, the buzz of the projector, the cold vodka in her hand, the fixation of her stare on the bar, the solidity of the cigarette in her hand, the silence of the audience behind her, a sign that they have moved on to some other art.

41

Robert Mapplethorpe is walking through the streets of Manhattan in 1986. He is walking to meet a friend for dinner. He is too busy to sleep. Although he needs sleep, there is no time to sleep. He will probably have sex with the friend he is meeting. Robert will take his picture first. He will suggest he take his picture and they will both know what that means.

At the restaurant, Robert is shown to his seat. He is an hour late, as this guy was expecting. It is all right. He has the time to wait for Robert Mapplethorpe.

Look, I can take your picture sometime, sure, just make an appointment with my secretary, Robert laughs.

They both laugh. The friend goes to the bathroom. Robert sits there.

The noise of the restaurant.

The rain falling in the street.

The creak of leather.

He plays with his French fries.

The friend returns.

I'm tired, Robert says.

Can't do it any more.

He's just teasing.

Look at the smile cut across his face.

———

Robert's collection includes: Lisa wearing a white veil, ghost. Finger pointing. Reclining. See the crease on her leg from her stockings – here she is wearing a bikini. Her arms, hands and feet are large. Stockings, gloves, garter belt. Her panties are pulled down. Stretch marks across her buttocks. Lisa looks in the mirror. Her left nipple is showing. In a plastic dress, astride a shaggy horse. Nike sneakers, workout girl, bent at the waist, angle of the sun against the wall. In Paris, on a balcony, Eiffel Tower in the distance. She wears a bathrobe. Standing against a white wall, in straw hat and bikini thong, elbow masking her breast, the shadow is caught on the wall. Astride a motorcycle, dressed in Tom of Finland leather. Her anus. Painted gold, she strikes a pose with her arms covering her face.

The portraits of Patti Smith include: Patti sitting wrapped in white muslin, lightning-strike tattoo on her knee, long dark hairs growing on her legs, dazed, dazzled. Bells around her ankle. Patti is listening to the statue, cupping her hand around her ear and leaning forward. Her hand against the white wall, looking back. First Patti holds the doves to her. Then she pushes them away. Patti with long, crimped hair and a wistful expression. The Patti Smith Group, and the doves are caged. Patti waves Robert away, she is laughing, smiling, the same dress as the shot with the doves. The photograph for Patti's album, *Horses*, white background, chain has come round to the centre, tie. Monogrammed shirt. The shirt is loose. Creases. Knots in her hair. Button undone. Patti sitting before a radiator, off-centre. The lines of the wooden floor and the radiators and the windows. The creases of her belly. The smooth line of her shoulders.

In 1988 Robert tells the interviewer that he couldn't do the leather pictures now. It wouldn't be right to do them now. No, he doesn't think about the future or the past. He thinks only of the present moment. In the present moment he is photographing classical statues and still-lives. He is coming back to inanimate form, light, shadow and physical structure. It's not about investigation any more, although he is still learning. He only photographs things that he wants to learn more about. He would like to get into film, he says. He would like to know more about that. He doesn't know what he will do next.

Mapplethorpe's flowers: A *Cactus Blossom*, tall, straight. Tall roses. *Babies' Breath*. White flowers lit from behind. *Bird of Paradise*. Giant daisies in a vase. Chrysanthemum in a vase, 1984, a flower placed in a vase. The vase is consuming the flower. *Jack in the Pulpit, Morgan's Hotel*, 1984, lily-looking, very straight.

In 1986 Robert takes a trip to East Hampton. He finds a secluded spot on the beach. He lies down in the sand and closes his eyes. It's not like the days of the golden bikinis or the royal portraits. Couples are walking their dogs on the beach. He listens to the ocean as he falls asleep. The sun is beating down on him as he lies still. As he is dreaming he has that feeling you get when you know. He knows something is terribly wrong. Something is happening to his body. Robert no longer has any defences. His camera has always been his protection. He would rather live the experience than photograph it. His camera was how he stayed safe. He wakes up. He has burnt himself head to toe in the sun. This is so easily done these days.

The sicker he gets, the harder he works. Reproductions of classical statues have been moved into Robert's studio. They stand against the wall staring with blank eyes into the room. Being reproductions, they possess no marks of age. They are perfectly white and clear. Robert dresses some in vest tops and scarves, the whiteness of their bodies, bright, illuminated by the studio lamps. He photographs some of them nude, moving slowly around the figures as he used to his live subjects. He cannot move as fast as he once did. He no longer looks out of the window. There is no time to look at anything that is not art.

Robert sits quietly in his rocking chair wearing his dressing gown and slippers. He chain-smokes, gazing into the middle distance. Everywhere, people are watching him, his assistants and secretaries. No one knows what's going on inside his head. He breathes in, he breathes out.

Robert's mother sends a priest to his apartment. She says Robert must prepare himself for the presence of God. He must ask forgiveness for all his sins. Robert invites the priest

into his apartment. They sit surrounded by Robert's ornaments, his collection of glass and antiquities, the many
objects that depict the devil, his photographs. Robert says
he likes to arrange things as all good Catholics do but he
does not seek religious comfort. There is no comfort for
him now. Robert will not confess his sins. These sins mean
that he was once alive.

42

Edmund looks into the window of the Museum of Sex. Two seats have been positioned beside the store's counter. The mic is bent low so that he can sit as he reads. There is a table, a glass, a pitcher of water. A cardboard cut-out of the Manhattan skyline has been placed behind the seats. A man is arranging chairs for the audience. Edmund enters the museum and approaches the counter.

I'm here to see the curator, he says.

Excuse me a moment, the young woman says. She picks up the telephone and dials a number.

She'll be down in a moment, she says.

There are a variety of objects for sale on the shelves. Pornographic playing cards, designer dildos, saucy lingerie, vintage pornography, lubricant, poppers, sexy aprons. He picks up a book about Japanese Shunga and flicks through the pages. He puts it down.

Mr White?

The curator is reaching for his hand.

Would you like a drink before we start? she says.

She shows him down a set of narrow stairs to a dark underground basement bar.

They approach the empty bar. A table along the back wall is filled with copies of Edmund's books. *City Boy* is the most prominent amongst them, the book he wrote about

New York. He is young in the cover photograph, his face in his hand.

What would you like? the curator asks.

Just water, thank you.

Have you been here before?

No, he says. I wonder how you can have a museum about sex. Is it already dead?

The curator laughs. Far from it, she says.

She hands him a menu from the bar, a list of aphrodisiac cocktails and a schedule for sex workshops, classes on how to give the perfect blow job, stripping classes, discussion forums.

It's about education, she says.

I wrote *The Joy of Gay Sex*, he says.

Yes. You're a pioneer.

Am I?

She leads him into the museum.

On the second floor there is an exhibition about sex in the digital age.

Have a look around, she says. Enjoy yourself.

A wall is filled with pictures, a full list of fetishes: shoes, grannies, baby dress-up, leather, food, role-play, bi, tri, watersports, instruments, outdoors, cars, enclosed spaces. A screen shows couples fucking on CCTV: in an office, in a staff room, in an elevator, in a hospital, in a telephone booth. This is what it means to be a voyeur, to be looking from above. Edmund has seen his fair share of this. He has seen it in the flesh. He has lived it.

Many people don't understand sex, the curator says.

Even in this country, people are afraid to ask. We at the museum want it to be transparent. We want people to know as much as possible. We have tried to make the museum as open as we can. For a long time the entrance was on 27th Street. We moved the entrance to Fifth Avenue and put in large windows so that people could see what we were doing. We're renovating the upper floors so that we can display more of our permanent collection. We're renovating the bar to attract a larger custom. Because we are not funded with public money we can pretty much do whatever we like, but it also means that we have to fund ourselves, and so the bar and the store are important. We also run courses, which you have seen.

Edmund is watching a video on a loop. A man mounts a woman who is lying back on a small sofa in an office. Her legs kick as the man thrusts. The video loops. Edmund sips his water.

Edmund listens to his summarized life. He doesn't want to hear it now.

It is an honour to be here, he says.

Piers.

High Line.

Bryant Park.

Times Square.

Tonight, I will read a passage from my new book.

He describes his entrance to the city, his temporary apartment, all the places he has seen. He describes himself.

I came here following the man I loved and ended up falling in love with the city, he reads.

But he feels the awkwardness of now. None of this is sitting correctly. The faces in the audience are very young. These people are from another world. They want to live in this city even though it is so difficult. They believe they are a part of a story that really ended long ago. Look, they are smiling, they are happy about it. But they must return to the outer boroughs when this night has ended because they can't afford to live in Manhattan. The whole time they are looking from the outside towards the centre, from Brooklyn, Queens and New Jersey. They believe the city needs their presence. Edmund knows this isn't true. They have travelled here for the sake of old dreams. The people who dreamed them have already left.

A young boy is peering through the museum window. This boy is not allowed inside because the subject of the museum is inappropriate for children. Life has not begun for him yet. For the moment, he is spared the anguish of physical love. He looks through the glass at Edmund White. Edmund doesn't know what he sees. Perhaps he is looking at the cardboard backdrop of New York City propped behind Edmund. It is the past, a movie set. It is a panel from a comic book. The boy is standing in the city but he doesn't know that yet. The city is out there, behind him, not in here with Edmund.

After the reading, Edmund signs many books. He asks his audience to spell their names. He writes their names in the books, crossing out his own printed name to sign instead.

43

Jane is walking up to a tenth-floor apartment in 1959. A woman is waiting for her at the top of the stairs. She is smiling, recognizing the extent of the climb. She welcomes Jane in and asks her to sit.

I wanted a new kitchen and a view of the city, she says. When they told me I was being moved I thought, finally, somewhere clean. I thought about the people uptown in the Plaza and the sights they must see through their windows. Now I can see the city, but I can't see my kids. I miss my old tenement, Mrs Jacobs. The windows were left open in the summer. I knew all my neighbours. I don't any more. The gangs that hang around down there are dangerous. No one comes to repair the lights. I used to have a friend in the next tower block. Look, Mrs Jacobs, in that window, the second floor down from the top and three windows across from the left, that's where my friend used to hang a red handkerchief to signal when she wanted me to come up for coffee. If it was up then I went out, down the stairs and across the grass. I walked up the stairs because the elevator was always broken. I knocked three times on her door so that she knew it was me. She's moved away now. I don't know where. I went over one day and she had gone. She didn't tell anybody where she went. Now I live here alone with my kids. Sometimes I wonder what it would be like to live in the suburbs in a white detached house with a wrap-around porch and a garden. I would sit on the porch and mend clothes there. My kids would play in the grass.

JONES BEACH, 2013

A man and woman are sitting on the sand beside a trash-can. The summer hasn't started yet. They watch seagulls beating their wings against the wind. Red flags mark the area within which it is safe to swim. A few children are throwing inflatable rafts onto the water and jumping on. Lifeguards watch, unconcerned, from high posts. The man and woman get up and walk to the West Bath House. The fast-food kiosks are faded, closed. The linoleum floor is stained and cracked. The woman looks up at the chandeliers from yesteryear hanging from the ceiling and imagines what this place must have looked like in the past. A janitor who has been mopping the floor straightens up and says, We're not open yet. Come back next week.

They go outside.

Why bring me here when it's closed? she asks.

Next week will be too crowded. Come on.

They sneak up the stairs that lead to the empty restaurant. Through the window they see chipped plastic chairs and Formica tables. Laminated menus lie in a pile by the door.

Was this place ever good? she says.

Beats me.

Over the wall they see dry swimming pools. The woman takes a photograph with her camera. They run down the steps. They are looking for a suitable secluded space. There are many to choose from, it seems. Along the boardwalk are scuffed basketball courts, volleyball courts, the faded fake grass of a pitch-and-putt course. The trashcans that line the boardwalk are designed in the style of ship vents made for luxury cruises. The paint on the handrails is chipped and spotted with gum. The boardwalk curves along the shore. It is empty except for the man and the woman. They are holding hands and looking about. They feel they are the only survivors of a natural disaster. It is impossible to imagine this place teeming with people. The display signs show pictures from the 1930s, a woman in a generous bathing suit and swimming hat, teetering on the edge of a diving board. The auditorium they come to is very small. In the distance they can see the new stadium built far away from the beach. A sound-check is being performed, getting ready for the first day of the season. They listen to the beat of a single drum. The woman kisses the man and leads him through the stage door to a dark corridor. Off the corridor are two dank rooms containing overturned plastic chairs. Seagulls call and beat their wings as the couple put their heads around the door. The man presses the woman against the cold, wet wall. She pushes him away.

Not here, she says. This whole place is wide open.

In the refreshment stand, a few beach-goers are lining up for French fries and slices of pizza. Giant sauce bottles line a dirty window ledge. There are vending machines, change machines. The floor is very dirty.

Further along the boardwalk is the East Bath House,

which is also closed. They walk up the flight of stairs to the upper floor where beach recliners are lined up in the shade.

Well? he says, lying out on one of the recliners and crossing his hands behind his head. He smiles. Come get me, he says.

Be serious, she says. She looks out at the ocean. There is a cold breeze now. She wants to feel the sun. They stay here awhile.

They walk back to the main entrance where families are posing for photographs before the Jones Beach sign. She takes a photograph of it too, then of the original black iron silhouettes of comical figures, a man holding a beach umbrella to advertise beach equipment, a woman striding off to change her clothes. They wait for the bus at the beach entrance. She sticks her legs into the sunshine. A man wearing dirty clothes asks them for money. When the bus comes they climb aboard and walk to the back seat. They are the only passengers aboard. The bus drives them back along the parkway. They look out at the ocean.

You always take me to the best places, she says.

He laughs and holds her hand. She lets him. They close their eyes. They sleep all the way back to Manhattan.

In the photograph, Laurie Anderson sleeps on the beach, lying on the smooth sand. Coney Island amusements loom in the distance. Her ankles are crossed. Eyes closed.

In the photograph, Laurie Anderson sleeps in the courtroom. She wears a hat and a thick overcoat. She sits pressed up against the wall. She has made herself small.

Beside each photograph is a description taken from the notebook in which Laurie Anderson wrote after she woke. The first thing she did when she woke up was to write down her dreams.

Laurie Anderson is changed by outdoor spaces.

It's not the place where she sleeps that's important but the things she records as she is dreaming, or after she has dreamt, or before, or when she is about to dream. Then it is what is left on the page that counts and not the sleeping as such. Though the sleeping has something to do with it because without the sleeping there would be no dreaming.

—

She is travelling all over New York, not just to Coney Island to sleep on the beach, and not just to the subway station, and not just to the afternoon court. She is interested in the line between the conscious and the unconscious. She wants to sustain the unconscious for as long as she can, but, of course, when she is asleep she is waiting to wake.

She feels under surveillance. This is because she is sleeping in public spaces. People are watching her as she sleeps. You could call the sequence 'The Sleepers' because there is more than one. When she is awake she looks at the photographs of herself sleeping. The city, too, is sleeping. There are no other people. The beach is empty. The courtroom scene is happening way away from the frame and you can't see the people.

44

The reporter follows the directions he's been given from the subway station, down a deserted residential street to the beach. The wind buffets him, cuffs him as he walks. He can't see the clear line of the tide due to the spray and mist hanging in the air. He checks his notebook as best as he can in such conditions, holding it in the shelter of an elbow crook. He walks along the beach to where he can see a line of beach cabins through the sea mist. He squints his eyes against the cold air. The boarded-up cabins are in need of restoration for the paint has begun to peel and crack. He continues along the beach but he can't see the houses he is looking for. He has been told this is where the residents are being housed, somewhere close to the beach. He makes his way past the cabins. He sees something in the corner of his eye as he passes. He looks at what it is – a girl of about six wrapped in a bed sheet, watching him – and he thinks he must be imagining things.

Where did you come from? he says.

She doesn't seem to understand.

Do you live around here? he says.

She doesn't move.

Where's your mom and dad? he says. Do you live around here?

She points to the cabin.

No, he says. Where do you live?

She points to the cabin.

You live there?

She nods.

Where is your family?

She points to the cabin.

The reporter knocks hard on the door of the cabin. He knocks again and pushes his nose against the windowpane. A young boy's face appears in the window and the reporter jumps back. He knocks on the door again.

Hello. Who's in there?

The front door opens and a man's face appears in the gap.

What do you want?

The little girl pushes past the reporter and runs into the cabin. The reporter sees other children sitting under blankets on the floor. The man slams the door.

Hello? Mister? Look, I've come to ask you a few questions for the paper. Will you talk to me, Mister?

45

Bucke wakes to the sound of low conversation. He opens his eyes. A young man is sitting beside Walt. Bucke closes his eyes and pretends to sleep. He cannot hear what they are saying. Always there is the sound of this train moving forward. Walt laughs. Bucke imagines his full weight tipping forward. Bucke opens his eyes. Walt sees him watching.

Say hello to my new friend, Walt says.

Bucke sits up and nods in greeting.

Walt seems a little drunk. He seems giddy. His cheeks are flushed. He has unbuttoned his shirt. His breakfast remains uneaten on the table. What is this, now? Now that we are getting close another man is here.

This man is from New York, Walt says. Explain to him what you have written. Come now, Bucke. What do you have to say for yourself?

It isn't ready, Bucke says. But I'll have it before we arrive.

Twelve hours, the man says.

Twelve?

Bucke shifts in his seat.

46

Jane rides her bicycle to the East Village, where she has arranged to interview another woman for her book. It is 1959.

She wheels her bike into a narrow alleyway and chains it to a drainpipe. The space is filled with ferns and geraniums, pebbles and polished shells. A jungle, a garden, created by this woman's own hands.

Jane pushes open the door and climbs the dingy staircase to the second floor. The corridor smells of damp and garlic. She knocks on the door to number 3.

The door is opened by a young woman in her thirties. She is wearing a pretty floral dress and a headscarf. She takes a long inhale of smoke from a cigarette, and says, Jane?

Jane smiles.

Please come in, the woman says.

Jane enters the studio apartment, where every surface is lined with books and pot plants, the shelves, tables, beside the stove, and hanging baskets hang from the ceiling. Through the fog of cigarette smoke the woman hands Jane a drink. Jane smiles and takes a cautious sip. The woman sits on her unmade bed and begins her story.

They say it's better to have your own private garden, the young woman says. They say it's better to have a seven-foot fence and a designated driveway. They say it's better never to walk the streets. You don't have a choice in the suburbs because in the suburbs there's nowhere to go. There are no restaurants or cafeterias. There are no squares or sidewalks, even. Once, I went out for a walk and I saw a woman I'd seen before at the local school. I didn't want to stop and talk. I'd gone for a walk to be by myself. But what was I supposed to do? I couldn't pretend I hadn't seen her. I couldn't turn around and walk the other way. So I said good morning and I asked her about her children, and she said Oh, they're fine, fine. Then she asked me about my children and I told her they were fine. Then we just stood there not knowing what to say. If we had been in the city I might have suggested we get a cup of coffee or a bite to eat somewhere but there was nothing like that there, only the diner on the freeway and that was too far to walk. I did the only thing I could do and invited her back to my house, and she said fine.

As we entered the hall I thought, This is it. I am laying my secrets out on the table. Here is a woman I hardly know standing in my house.

In the kitchen, I delayed conversation as best I could. I played with the coffee grinder and the filter machine. I struggled to find something to say. We talked about the things we had in common. We had both moved here from out west. Neither of us was close to our families. I wanted to say, Hey, let's get out of here. The city isn't far away. I thought about how it would feel to arrive in New York. We could start a new life, my new friend and I. I wanted to say,

They would never find us. Instead, I said, I worry about my husband working late in the city. I worry about him coming home late at night. I worry about the times when he doesn't come home at all. I worry about my kids. They don't talk to me any more. I used to live in a studio apartment in the city. I remember sleeping and dreaming in that one room. I remember falling into it late at night with friends. There was no sense of the future or the past then. But now I am this person. Now I am a wife and a mother. Now I am this stranger's friend. If the two of us had been sitting somewhere in the city something would have happened to break our concentration – a siren, a beggar passing the window of the cafe, a beautiful woman walking by. We would be reminded that our problems were only very small. These people you see all around you, in the street, in the diner – they all have lives. But in suburbia, there are no distractions. There are only other houses that look the same as yours. My coffee guest thinks I am the only way out of her situation. My problems are a distraction from hers. I have become the siren in the street, the beggar passing the window where we are sitting, the beautiful woman walking by. She peered at me over the rim of her coffee mug. She was waiting for me to speak but I couldn't. I just sat there looking at her, watching her. What was I supposed to say? Then I remembered something that had happened.

A few months before that day, I was at home as usual. My kids came home from school and ran straight up to their rooms. My husband came home from work and sat down in his chair in the den as usual. The rooms and corridors of the house were silent. The TV flickered in the corner of the room, on but not watched by anyone. My husband, sitting in the chair, was dozing. I was standing in the hallway watching him. I was sure there must be something I needed to do but there was nothing. I could not go out. There was nowhere to go. I could take the car but where would I drive? I wasn't even sure I could find the freeway. The scene in front of me came from the past. I was a child standing in the hallway of my childhood home and the man sitting in his favourite chair was my father, and the children sleeping upstairs were my brother and sister. I thought, You could have moved away to the city. You could have shared a place with your friend from college. You could have jumped on a bus and made your own way. You could have walked the streets, walked all day and all night and no one would have cared. You would have been invisible to others yet entirely known to yourself. You would have made something of yourself. You would have turned yourself into a work of art, and this is what people would have seen, everything that you promised to be from such a young age, standing there on a street in the city. You could have been something. You would not be this woman who confuses time.

I made dinner. I came through to tell my husband it was ready. He was already asleep in his chair. I looked out of the window. I saw the dark expanse of lawn, the shadow of sycamore trees, my son's bedroom light. The street was black.

I took the car keys.

The car was very cold. I did not know how far I would go. I hoped to see a sign for the station, and I did. I found the station. I parked the car. I just wanted to see. I wanted to stand on the platform and watch the train pull in. The guard said I couldn't enter without a ticket, so I bought a ticket. I stood on the platform.

I suddenly remembered my mother used to sit and stare at the living-room wall. I always thought that when she did this it was because she was thinking something through from start to finish. I thought I must not break her concentration, as one must never wake a sleepwalker. I thought my mother would stop as soon as she solved the problem. But the silences became longer and I thought, I've left it too long. I should have done this sooner. I should have known to try.

The train approached. People got off the train. They pushed past me. I climbed aboard. I stood in the entrance. I couldn't do it. I climbed back down. The train left.

I didn't tell my houseguest this. I talked about other things instead, about the local school, about the teachers that neither of us liked. We talked this way for a half-hour more then she said goodbye and left the house. I hadn't remembered my attempted escape until that afternoon. I would not have thought about it had it not been for this stranger. Within a month, I had moved to the city. I found this place. A great weight has been lifted off my shoulders, Mrs Jacobs. As you can see, moving here has been a great success. The city has a lot to offer a single woman like me.

WEST 23RD STREET (1971)

Patti Smith's room contains dresses, lipstick, books of poetry, sheets of paper, shoes, pencils, crayons, paint pots, brushes, underwear, bed sheets pulled off the bed, in a tussle with a dressing-gown belt, sheet music – Bob Dylan, his face in close-up, looking humble – the stuffing from a feather pillow, grey feather boa (someone else's), guitar strings, china plates filled with cigarette butts, bottles of piss lining the wall, catching sunlight, Twinkie wrappers, plastic sandwich casings, extra blanket lying on the floor like a picnic rug, no food, typewriter on the floor at the end of the mattress; one night she got her feet stuck in it. Posters on the greying walls – Dylan, Hendrix, King – an altar set up by the window, Robert's idea, never used it, sick of the religion, can't create art in a museum or a factory, must come from the throw-up of everyday life, which is this, her life, strewn across the floor. She once returned and didn't know whether she had been burgled or not until she saw the broken window. Robert's leather jacket was missing, Robert's favourite, so upset. Then they found the jacket on the fire escape – Didn't they want my jacket, Patti? She consoled him, said the burglar was probably disturbed. It'll be worth a million bucks some day, he said. No kidding, said Patti, sick of the money, the talk of money, the lack of money, the lack of food, the lack of art, the art all over the floor, the neatness of art in the museums, which is nothing, which isn't her and isn't him, which isn't nothing but a pretty picture, and she's going crazy living like this, there is too much of her here, there is no restraint, there is nobody telling her no, she is yes all the time, she says yes, and they say yes, and it does no fucking good. It isn't good, this saying yes to everybody, this incessant consent, implied, she's slipped in, she's slipped down, she is slipping down, she's Alice, she's the Queen, the rabbit, the fucking pocket watch, she's the tie that binds them all together, she's pulled hard in a knot and can't be untied from this, she's Houdini getting old and tired of the trick knots and the chains and the locks, because what good is breaking out of places? This is just a way to get out of tidying your room, Patti, says Robert. He has a grin on his face because he has already tidied his and it's not yet noon. I'm going out, he says. She throws her pillow, misses him, misses him completely, knocks over a bottle of piss. Piss and Dylan meet like sweethearts.

47

Manhattan means options, Robert Mapplethorpe says. I can be creative here; I can do anything. But it's not easy. There's incredible pressure. Everything in New York is expensive. This means you have to be productive all the time.

He is talking to a journalist in his home. Lined along the walls behind him is his glass collection, and many objects on shelves: wooden figurines, a figure of the devil. He is calm while he is talking. His hands are interlaced neatly on his lap. The sweater he is wearing is thick, bulky. He speaks slowly, doesn't get excited.

An artist has to be immersed in his own time, he says. Art is a statement of the moment it is made. Art should look to the future but it is not about the future. Art should be so accurate that most people don't see it. My life began in the summer of 1969. Before that I didn't exist. I'm not so excited about what's going on in the arts today. I don't want today's paintings. Perhaps I'm just old fashioned.

He smiles.

Robert rides the elevator to the top floor of the Whitney Museum of Art in 1988. The curators are waiting to greet him there. They rush to help him out of the elevator. He walks unaided past them all. He stands before a wall of photographs and looks at his self-portrait. It shows a skull-topped cane in the foreground and his blurred face behind. He doesn't feel he is this man.

They are asking him about the Perfect Moment.

Robert is nodding but he is thinking, Which one? The one when I picked up a camera for the first time, the one when I met Patti Smith, the one when I met Sam Wagstaff, the one when I was told I would die, the moment of my death?

Is there anything you would like us to change? they ask.

Black frames, white mounts, black and white photographs. Dancers, black and white – evening dress. Lisa Lyon. Flower. Breast. Statue. Ajitto. Andy Warhol. Christ. Wig. Flower. Stretched man. Fish on paper. Coral sea. Grapes. Ben Sherman and Ken Moody. Ajitto on a plinth. Coloured flowers. Rippled muscle, shown in quarters. Flowers. Vases. Red mount. Milton Moore. Cock. Robert Mapplethorpe wearing make-up. Stars. Crosses. Whip. Cock on a marble slab. Patti Smith. Moody. Moody. Man with dagger. Louise Bourgeois. Naked Patti Smith and a radiator. Patti is young. Andy Warhol. Neck brace. Coloured faces. Cock. Arnold Schwarzenegger. Breast.

He is looking at the photographs. These people have selected the pictures and organized them in a line. Here is his life.

I need to go, he says.

In the studio Robert tells Laurie Anderson to look down at the ground.

Look right down. Now close your eyes. Now open them. Now put your hands against your face. Frame your face with your hands. Look down again. Good.

Robert takes her picture. She is looking away. Her eyes are closed.

You wouldn't want to change one thing about this picture, he says. Just look at how beautiful she is.

Laurie Anderson leaves the studio and crosses Bond Street. She walks west along it towards Broadway. Posed, she feels serene, not like the city at all, which is chaotic. She turns right onto Broadway. The day has been cordoned off but Laurie Anderson is free. There is a rope around life. She knows Robert looks for evidence of life through his studio window, down on the street.

48

Edmund is watching couples tango dancing in Central Park. Their bodies collapse into one another. Their moves are deliberately slow. The gravel beneath them is marked by the swivel of pivoting feet. On the surrounding benches people lean in to watch. The dancers know where other couples are. Together, they are an active mass. They twist and step together. This is a pleasant day. The women in the group are wearing blouses, jeans and sensible shoes. The old men dance with their eyes closed. They hold their partner's hands gently. This is the centre of Manhattan Island. The centre is the heart. The heart is the organ of love. Edmund wants the constant pressure of another body against his, not the rough and tumble of the city, avoiding people coming his way as he walks down the street. Not the elbow in the back on the subway or the grip of a hand on the back of a seat, or the nudging to be next in line – these are all temporary shunts. What he wants is constant pressure.

Edmund walks towards the bandstand, towards another crowd. People are surrounding a group of men beating African drums. The audience is clapping and stamping to the beat. Children are dancing.

This park used to be dark and barren. This was where all the unwanted people came. There was no grass left at that time. The benches had been vandalized and fences were broken. There were no park lanterns and no hansom-cab rides. The fountains were dry and stood abandoned. There were no boats sailing on the lake. The water in the lake was poisoned and dangerous. Central Park has never been a natural space. It was designed from the outset. It was planned and organized.

In the park, things could go one way or the other. Here, it would only take a slight dip and things would go back to the way they were, the rusted gates and the barren lawns, the dried-up fountains and the vandalized restrooms, the lights going out, one by one, people leaving. What would happen then would be this: the men would pick up their drums and the park would stand empty. These children would be dead already. He has seen the barren lawns. He has brought lovers to this place. He has experienced vital exchanges. The movement between them took place in the dark. Nothing is ever fixed down, he thinks. This park is just another vision of mine. By being here, I am walking through a dream. This is a video caught on a loop. There are no seams to break the show; it will continue, just the same. Edmund has lived this day a thousand times. He has already described it and written it down. He and the park are exactly the same. They created themselves out of a design but this design has not always been well maintained.

Couples are rowing boats on the man-made lake. Edmund walks to where the great boulders are. They are another fabrication. He scrambles to the top. From here the line of truth is obvious. The hard line of the outer shore of the lake and the swoop and swerve of the shoreline, the pier where the boats are moored and the formation of this rock are things from a picture book. There is nothing to mar this vision. If this place were a man Edmund would think him too perfect. He would not excite Edmund White, though he should think him very beautiful. He wonders what he will leave behind when he dies. There are the stories in his books. Then there are the books themselves. I don't know how I will change, he thinks. This comes from wanting to write about New York. He looks at the city and he sees himself. But a man is not a city, thinks Edmund White. Once I am dead there will be no way to reform me – my body will lie deep in the ground and it cannot be changed. Perhaps he has no centre any more. Perhaps there is no way to fix him down. His lovers are mostly dead. For now he sits in Central Park.

He cannot now remember when he was young. Instead, he has a memory of a sunset. The sun had fallen behind the west side of Manhattan. It left a black silhouette, the Eldorado, visible above the reservoir. In the darkness he couldn't see the trash on the shoreline or the garbage floating in the water. It was in this extreme half-light that this city came alive. Edmund cannot imagine it happening now, the gradual falling of light, the blazing horizon. Instead, he imagines a light lit one moment and extinguished the next.

Edmund slips down from his rock and walks through

Strawberry Fields. Here, a man is selling watercolour portraits of John Lennon, peace badges and I♥NY T-shirts. Everyone in New York is in love, except him. Edmund walks quickly from the park.

49

The reporter has tracked Robert Moses's daughter down to a bench in Central Park. It is 1963. He sits down beside her and looks for the likeness of the father. He looks for the formidable man.

I thought it was strange for us all to get in a boat and sail from our home on Long Island, she says. I pictured every island going east getting smaller and smaller until it was nothing but a grain of sand. I thought of the country as a whole, how big America is. People told me my father was rebuilding New York. My father was going to save this city from itself, they said. They told me he knew where to put things. They said he liked things to be kept moving so he built the roads to get the cars moving, and he built the parks to get people moving. When we had a holiday we were always on the move. First into the boat with our luggage then sailing across the ocean to Fire Island. When I thought about it I thought of it ablaze, and when I saw it, I imagined the fire spreading from shore to shore along the strip of sand, and what would I do if I were there and trapped – well – Daddy would find a way to get us all moving. We camped on the beach. When the weather was bad we stayed in an abandoned beach house. We laid mattresses on the floor. We slept together in one room and we lit a fire in the hearth. We went out for long walks on the beach. There were shipwrecks on the shore. I remember playing hide and seek. We cooked fresh fish over the fire and we lay in the sand. We looked up at the stars. We were packed off to bed, the children and Mom, but he never went to bed. When everyone else was asleep I watched him come into the room then turn to leave again. I followed him. I watched him walk along the beach. I watched him unbutton his shirt and step out of his clothes. I watched him stride into the ocean. My father loves to swim. Did you know that?

50

Jane takes her seat in the front row of the conference room in 1961. Everyone is waiting for her to speak. She knows there are things beyond this city. She reminds herself she was not born here, but one can grow attached to things.

Jane, dear Jane – thank God you're here – have you seen the entourage?

Her friend points to the men sitting on the stage.

Her friend's bottom lip is trembling. Jane wants to tell her to get a grip. These are just men. They think this meeting is a mere formality. They have their speeches already prepared. They have planned to be out at lunch in half an hour. But their confidence is an advantage. Arrogant men never think they can be beaten.

How will you do it? Oh, how will you do it, Jane?

Jane pats her arm. There, there, she says. There, there.

What these men don't know is that Jane has already been to City Hall and she has already seen the expressway plans. She has recorded the dates of their proposals. She has made copies of these to hand out to the audience. The documents explain that the things they are about to say are lies. The men will say that there is nothing these people can do, that time has already passed and it cannot now be reclaimed. They will say that the moment for protest is already over. They will claim that these people have no

211

right of appeal. This is all fiction, of course. The time for protesting is not yet over. These men won't receive official authorization for another six weeks. They are planning what is known as premature severance, a way to nip the problem in the bud before the protesters become aware of their rights and organize themselves. They are counting on the fact that most people believe what they are told, particularly by men in suits.

Jane will not get up right away. She will allow them first to say their piece. It pays to be level-headed in moments like these. It pays to understand the possibilities of time. The women all around her are fluttering like birds but Jane is as calm as a stone. She has met this type of man before. They are nothing compared to her. Jane waits patiently for it all to begin.

51

Patti Smith is sitting on the floor of a white room in 2006. She is refusing to leave this room until the filmmaker has finished making his film.

She has barricaded herself in with all her possessions. They are relics. Objects build up over time, she says. These are just the things that are left.

She takes a tambourine from the wall.

Robert made this for my birthday, she says. But you don't want to know about this; you want me to talk about New York. I slept in parks and subway stations. I looked for jobs in restaurants and stores. I wasn't in danger because no one paid me any attention. No one was looking at this skinny kid walking around Manhattan. I used to pretend I was being filmed. I posed in the reflections of store windows and in the reflections of moving vehicles streaming up and down the avenues of the city and in subway car windows. I knew every pose of Modigliani's models, those pale, skinny women who were also his lovers, their narrow eyes and long jutting limbs, because they looked a lot like me.

It was a different world back then. You didn't think about being molested. People were happy to be in the city. People looked out for one other. People were watching when it counted. Kids complain to me all the time. They say, How do *I* do it, Patti? The city's too expensive now. I can't do what you did then. I say, Find a cheaper city. Move someplace else. Save up money to buy the time to make your art.

Patti opens a small wooden box beside her and pulls out a Polaroid of her and Robert Mapplethorpe standing in Coney Island when they were both young. She has a scarf around her head. She is dressed in white and squinting against the sun. Robert is dressed head to toe in black with a white scarf around his neck.

We all want souvenirs, she says. We want relics. I guess it's a Catholic thing. Objects take on the power of moments. This Polaroid became that as soon as I held it in my hand. All of the objects around me possess this power. That's why I don't ever have to leave this room.

She takes out an urn from a cabinet and holds it up for the camera.

I think the urn is Persian, she says.

She struggles to open the catch. She tips the grains into the palm of her hand.

These are Robert's remains, she says. They look more like pieces of shell. See how they catch the light? I take him with me places. We travel together. This is all that's left of him now. This is just a small part. Most of his remains are with his mother and father. You know, T. S. Eliot said that every generation translates for itself. You have to respect history whilst also breaking it apart. I think you have to learn to control it. This means forcing yourself to see. Is this what you're doing with your film?

Steven imagines Patti's bus drawing into Manhattan on her arrival. She looks at her reflection in the window as the bus moves on. She watches her own reflection as the city moves behind it.

We've all made a decision like that once in our lives, she says. You just need to do it and then it's done. All the hard work lay ahead of me then but what did I care? I was young, I was free. I had arrived. I had a vision of the future. That's how I've lived my life. That's me.

Steven once filmed Patti taking a rubbing from Allen Ginsberg's grave. The sheet of paper was a copy of a symbol that described a life. The charcoal dirtied her fingers. She brushed her fingers on the side of her pants. She took a photograph of the grave. This was another duplication.

Steven is recording everything because he doesn't know when the crucial scene will come. He has been doing this for ten years. For ten years he has been filming Patti Smith. He has found that she never veers off to the side and she never pretends. Sometimes it is as if he can see right through her to the other side of the room. Sometimes he thinks she can see into him. Love pours from her like light.

52

Al Smith visited Central Park Zoo after it closed up for the day. He entered through the side gate using the key that Moses had given him. He walked to the sea-lion pen. He looked at the sea lions swimming in the water, swimming without any urgency, just floating there. The pathways were clear. Night was descending. The animals dozed in their pens. A low hush fell over the park. He shouted at the penguins but they did not look at him. He roared at the lion. He knew a thing or two about them. You put your head right into the lion's mouth every time you stepped into City Hall.

Al Smith was appointed President of the Empire State Building in 1928. When the building was completed in 1931, Smith stood in his empty office one thousand feet up in the air. The corridors and offices of the building remained empty because no one could afford the midtown rent. Al Smith had become the president of nothing. He looked down at the city from his high window. As governor he had presided over millions of New Yorkers and then suddenly he governed just one hundred and two storeys of empty space. He sat in an empty room. He looked out across Manhattan. He wondered where all of the people were. He used to walk the city's streets. He knew everybody's names. But now he couldn't even make their figures out.

NEW FRIEND, 2015

A young woman sits on a bench in Tompkins Square Park. A man is playing ragtime tunes on a grand piano. An old man is lying on a bench. Tourists are looking through shopping bags. A teenage girl is talking on a cell phone. The young woman reads back what she has written in her notebook then crosses it out.

The young woman walks to a cafe beside the park and takes a seat in the window. She takes out the notebook from her purse, opens it out flat on the table. She takes out a pen from her purse and begins to write. She stops writing, distracted by a woman breastfeeding a child at a table outside. The woman has covered the baby's head with a scarf but the young woman can see the baby's cheek puff out as its mouth fills with milk.

The young woman walks west to Broadway. At the Strand she stops to look at the discounted books. The yellowing pages of the books are tattered, the covers bent. The subjects are not ones she is interested in. She wants to discover a book that will change her life. She looks through the stands thoroughly, and when she gets to the last stand, having found nothing, she turns around and looks through them all again. She will not go inside because she cannot afford to. She looks through the window at the merchandise. She has many books at home that she could trade. She sees the staff looking through old boxes of books.

To save the subway fare, she walks to the New York Public Library. She allows the guard to search her bag. She climbs the staircase, pauses to look at the etchings on display – ink drawings of Thoreau's Walden Pond – then continues the climb. The space echoes with the sound of heavy doors swinging open. Tourists in canvas shoes stand like cows. She walks past the issue desk and into the reading room. She chooses a desk and sits down. She opens her notebook and takes out her pen.

She eats her sandwich in Bryant Park, sitting on a step beside the fountain. Before her a great screen is being erected for an outside movie festival that is starting next week. It casts a shadow across her.

In the library she writes a series of passages describing the noises she can hear as she sits at her desk: the squeak of shoes on the polished floor, the slamming of books, fingers tapping keyboards, the clearing of throats, a wayward child running away from its guardian. This is not a story. It is not what she had planned to write. But this is all that is in her mind. She can hear the traffic out on the street. The windows are open so this is easy. Sirens wail. There are too many locations. If she moved to a different place she would hear other sounds, people playing sports in Central Park, traffic congestion at Columbus Circle, and so on.

―――

She meets friends in a bar below the High Line in Chelsea. They stand outside the bar to smoke. She listens to her friends talking but she says little herself. She sips her beer. When a next round is called for she pretends she hasn't heard. She is approached by a woman she has never met before. The woman tells her that she has moved to the city from Vermont. She is an artist but she doesn't know what to paint; she needs to find herself first. She is certain inspiration will come now that she's moved to New York City. She is living in Greenpoint in Brooklyn. She wants to move to Manhattan. She has taken a receptionist job at the Guggenheim. This will be good for her art. But she needs more money so she can move to Manhattan. Somewhere cool, she says. Like the Meatpacking District or the Lower East Side.

The party moves to a bar on West 23rd Street. The young woman smokes a cigarette outside. She is looking at the neon sign of the Chelsea Hotel. The couple smoking next to her are discussing art. The man has just had his first exhibition and he is complaining about the criticism he overheard in the gallery. The woman beside him is trying to calm him down – at least you've *had* an exhibition, she is saying. Stop being such an asshole. He storms into the bar.

He is an asshole, the woman says. He thinks he's the only person who's ever tried to express himself.

The young woman explains that she has come here to write.

That's cool, the woman says.

———

The two women arrange to meet at a cafe in Harlem. The young woman arrives half an hour early. She walks up the block to waste some time. She passes a congregation exiting a church, white suits and hats, newly polished shoes. She has tried to look casual as if this meeting doesn't matter: baggy jeans, sneakers. But she has brushed her hair and pinned it up and she is wearing lipstick. She turns and walks back to the cafe. The woman is not here yet. She goes in and takes a window seat. She opens her notebook. She looks for a long time at the blank page.

No good? The woman is standing before her.

No, she says.

Give it time.

They order coffee. They talk about everything. The new friend wanted to be a reporter but she's fallen off that path and ended up in environmental campaigning.

Some things have become more important, she says.

I'm not doing what I thought I would be doing, the young woman says. I don't know what I'm doing but that's all right. I don't have any money but that's not the problem. I need time to think, that's what it is. Every day something new happens here, and I feel new because of that. I don't know how many people I've been since I came here. I don't suppose that really matters. I don't know who I'll be when I go home.

Do you have to go home? the woman says with a smile.

They quit their apartments to rent a small studio together in Prospect Heights. They often walk together through

Prospect Park. The new friend tells the young woman all about the plants growing there. They spend many Sunday afternoons walking through Brooklyn. The new friend likes to read literature aloud. She says it will inspire the young woman to write. She reads extracts from poems from the screen of her phone. They like to walk through Cobble Hill, where there are trees and the streets are quiet. They walk to Brooklyn Heights and look across the river at Manhattan.

Walt Whitman used to live round here somewhere, the new friend says. I don't know where, exactly.

They eat fruit in the Cobble Hill Park and watch the couples and women with strollers walking through. When they come here at night they eat slices of pizza and watch the fireflies dance.

They don't have a lot of money but they know all the cheap places to eat. They avoid the organic grocers and they buy food that's past its use-by date. They don't have a TV and so don't pay for cable. They use the Internet for free at the Brooklyn Library. When they go out with friends they order a beer, which they share, then they top the bottle up with liquor brought from home. They go to museums when the entrance is free, and never at any other time. When they are out walking they take a packed lunch. There are many free concerts in the summer. The young woman does not write as much as she used to but when she does write she is pleased with the improvement. Her friend reads out the young woman's writing as they walk through Brooklyn.

Sometimes the young woman forgets that the writing is her own. The young woman sends work to magazines and a couple of pieces are published. When bills are due, they cut right back, preparing as one might for battle. They stock up on food and make it last. They turn leftovers into soups and bulk meals out with bread or rice. They are boosted by the changing of the seasons. The streets that have become so familiar transform, and so do they. They can't remember a time when they didn't know each other. They watch movies for free on the High Line in the summer. They take up dancing by copying couples in Central Park. When they walk through Chelsea they always walk along 23rd Street. They laugh about the artist the new friend used to know. They like to describe how much the city has changed throughout their friendship, as if the city didn't exist before this event. The new friend explains it like a scientific formula – certain conditions need to exist before change can occur. All love is a product of changing environmental forces, the friend says. And art can't exist without love.

53

Between 1955 and 1969 Robert Moses builds the Lincoln Center for the Performing Arts. He brings together the Metropolitan Opera, the New York Philharmonic, the New York Public Library for the Performing Arts and the Juilliard School.

To build this centre he evicts over ten thousand people. Moving this many people isn't easy. There are many protests and petitions, but Moses gets it done.

You theoretically ought to negotiate with every individual until he is happy, Moses says. Do you imagine building anything under those conditions?

After the centre is completed, the real-estate value in the area soars.

You can't tell me that the neighbourhood isn't happy now, says Moses.

54

Walt changes his position in the carriage, following the angle of the sun. He remembers scenes from his past. The war is over. His mother is dead. And he is here on this train. He is travelling to New York. They will arrive there soon. His friend is writing another book. Bucke has written many pages. He has torn the pages from his notebooks. They are placed beside Bucke upon the seat. Walt's whole life, written by somebody else, is lying there.

I want to talk about Long Island, Walt says. Now listen to me, Bucke. I stood on the shoreline where shipwrecks littered the sand. I watched the men who were bathing there. I sat in the sun. I took off all of my clothes. The men were bathing and diving into the water. They were so alive. I watched them. The tide was coming in. It would be a good hour before it reached me, but it would come. I ripped the sheet from the book, folded it and tucked it under my pile of clothes. I remembered my ancestors who I have never known. I had the impression that life was eternal. My life stretched out before me like a never-ending line in the sand and I could sense the universe. I walked out and waded in the ocean. I went out further and began to swim. I swam until I could not touch the ground. I floated and looked up at the sky and back at the beach where the bathers were dressing.

Walt once visited Bucke in Ontario. Walt never kept his room tidy. Instead of folding his clothes neatly in the drawers, he laid them out on the bed and chairs. He set his books and papers out on the tables and on the floor but never in the bureau provided. He spread himself throughout the house. He slept very late. When he woke he took an age to rouse himself. He did not dress until the afternoon. He walked about the house in his underclothes then he demanded lunch. He insisted that everyone come out for walks outdoors even though their days were already well established. They followed him through the garden and out into the pasture, over fences, through brooks, into the wilderness. The world was suddenly alive. The flowers smelt sweeter and the sun was hotter. The brook was icy cold. The season, always summer. Walt ripped pages out of books and stuffed them into his shirt pocket. This was to reduce the weight of what he must carry.

When is he leaving? asked Mrs Bucke.

I don't know, said Bucke.

Haven't you asked him?

Bucke wanted to say, I would have him here for ever if I could.

He can't stay, said Mrs Bucke. I can't stand it. He's always lying about the house and ripping up our books. This man is unashamed of his reproductive organs. And I don't think he's much of a poet.

Bucke found Walt crouching over the remnants of books at the bottom of the garden. He was trying to get at something. Whatever it was, it was something he was not getting.

I need to speak with you, said Bucke.

I can find no order here, said Walt. I would do better in the middle of a war where nothing is certain.

How Bucke wanted to keep him there with him. What makes us want to possess the things we love? He has seen it in the daguerreotypes and photographs, images of loved ones framed and worn on the person or hung on the wall – a mother, a father, a deceased child, a soldier. He has seen photographs of Walt. These images depict his friend yet they do not adequately communicate his animated form. The Walt who is alive is always moving and changing. These pictures only show what existed once.

Bucke is reading alone in the carriage. He is taking a break from his story. He tries to think of his wife and his children. He will be very happy to see them again. He has lived away from them for too long. They are his family, his flesh and blood. But when he sees Walt standing in the corridor laughing with the porter his heart beats wildly. He thinks about Walt writing those letters for the soldiers during the war, sitting in their tents and writing the words of other men, writing down their hopes and dreams. How lucky they were to have him so close.

The Variations

(2011)

EDWARD MAPPLETHORPE

The walls of the Foley Gallery are lined with prints of abstract swirls and lines in colours of brown, black, white, grey and gold.

The artist Edward Mapplethorpe is telling an interviewer, I am able to achieve the colour by scattering light. It is all about process.

These pictures do not depict anything from Edward's real life. These Mapplethorpes are organic forms.

These pictures have more in common with painting than with photography, Edward says. Here, one is observing the process of art and not just its final presentation. Here, there are no faces, bodies or landscapes. There is nothing recognizable. There is only colour, form and process.

In the centre of the room, Patti Smith is giving an interview to a journalist. She is explaining that she always knew Edward would become an artist. When she and Robert visited him in Floral Park, she talked to Edward about art and his future.

Edward says, These pictures are made by using the photographic process as the subject. Not just as a way to develop the photograph. In effect, this is not photography at all because the process is not complete. There is no camera here and there is no subject. There is only methodology. This is all done in the darkroom. Here, there is no reality to depict. The shapes are confusing. They are a product of the process, he says. Here, there is nothing more to see. There is no story to describe. There is no story.

I had the idea on September 11th, says Edward. It was something to do with seeing the towers inside out. I saw colours, shapes and process. I saw all the subjects I had ever depicted in my photographs and suddenly there was a definite thick black line between then and now – I decided I wouldn't go back. I would replicate something of this effect in my studio.

He remembers how it all began.

Riding the subway into Manhattan, staring out the window at Queens sailing by, the fading fall light, the pink hue of apartment towers, the train plunging deep underground, Edward's face reflected in the window, a shadow of Robert's.

Edward thinks, We came from the same place, Robert and I. These photographs do not depict Robert but Robert is contained within all of them. On the information pamphlet Edward blocks out the word 'Robert' and reads 'Mapplethorpe'.

When he stayed in Robert's Bond Street apartment, he felt misplaced. The chicken-wire cage cast a shadow across the floor. Streetlight flooded the room. He bathed in dirty light. He was planning his own exhibition then. He could see it all perfectly, his own crisp, clear style.

Robert once asked him to change his name.

They were eating together in a diner. Edward named everything he could see –

table,

glass,

pitcher,

brother.

It's not such a big deal for you. It's not as if you are anybody yet, said Robert. Why don't you take another name? Take Mom's name. Why don't you take Maxey? Take Maxey. No one has done anything with Maxey. You're not going to screw this up for me. I have worked too fucking hard to make a name for myself. Don't you want to be independent? Don't you want to do something on your own?

But it's my name, Edward said.

You should take Maxey. Maxey suits you. Mom would want you to have it. Look, everyone is happy with Maxey. I can't change my name. I'm already a Mapplethorpe. I was a Mapplethorpe before you were born.

When Edward wrote a college thesis about his brother, he adopted an objective, critical tone but he never could separate himself from the name. When Edward walked into the diner that morning he was Edward Mapplethorpe but he walked out of it Ed Maxey.

I saw it on the news, says Edward. A dirty cloud falling on New York. It did not settle on the ground. It did not end. I tried to breathe. My breath mixed with other fragments in the air, all the elements and particles, all the dirt and lint that had been swept up from the ground. There is only ever process. I saw it in the swirls of dust. I saw it in the way that every part was falling as it should, as its weight allowed, every desk, chair, every shard of glass, every piece of paper, every handbag, shoe, was falling completely in accordance with the laws of physics, and I was looking at the result of those laws, the result of how things collide. There would never be an end because the dust would never settle. No one would ever be able to trace the lines back, to find a beginning. And there was no end. Something shifted in me.

Edward says, I am getting my life back on track. This is my time now. There is so much I want to do. I went off the rails there for a while. But now I'm right back where I should be. There have been ups and downs, sure. I was an addict. But that's all in the past. I have put all of that behind me. I am working harder than ever, creating, you know? I'm Edward Mapplethorpe again.

Photography is interesting, Edward says. Because it shows something that once existed. A photograph preserves a moment in time. A photograph is a window into someone else's life but that moment no longer exists.

What was it like being Robert Mapplethorpe's brother? the interviewer asks.

55

The videotape lies on top of the VCR. The handwritten label reads *The Perfect Moment*. Robert looks at his silhouette in the television screen. There is his outline in the glass but not the detail of his features. Dandruff floats down onto his lap. He licks his dry lips.

You wanna watch a film? his assistant asks.

She puts the tape into the machine and switches it on.

What message do people have for Robert? What do they think of Robert Mapplethorpe? What do they want to share with him?

Man: He's sensuous. Of our time. It's great to see Robert's work. Best wishes.

Woman: I've seen your work for many years but I think they touched me most tonight. Thank you for everything.

Man: I applaud Robert's courage in realizing his own vision, and I applaud his aesthetic, which is impeccable. One of the greatest photographers of this century.

Woman: One of the sexiest people that ever existed.

Group: Robert, congratulations, and our thoughts are with you.

There is a shot of Robert's self-portraits – the skull cane, Robert's eyes, Robert with the whip up his ass.

It's like watching my own funeral, he says.

—

In the hospital Robert has his own room with a TV. The nurse sets a vase of flowers on his bedside table. The card reads *With Love, from Mom and Dad.* But his mom is also ill. This means it must have been his father who sent the flowers. It must have been his father who wrote the card.

The nurse comes back.

I'm sorry, she says. These flowers were meant for another patient.

She takes them away. He watches them go.

56

The film Edmund is watching in the Museum of the City of New York is describing the construction of Brooklyn Bridge in the late nineteenth century.

Brooklyn Bridge represents not an external 'thing' but an internal process, an act of consciousness, the narration says. *It shows the ambition of human will.*

Next, the building of the Empire State Building in 1931, steel beams swinging into place, the skyward ballet of the men who fixed them, standing on tiptoes on the edges of beams and hammering bolts into place. The men in the picture are smiling as they eat their lunch sitting on beams, high in the air. Now the men are gone but the building remains.

The manufacturing of weapons during the Second World War and prosperity, then the slump, waning New York, economic decline – Edmund's era – the 1970s – the famous newspaper headline: *Ford to City: Drop Dead*.

The construction of the World Trade Center, monoliths balanced on impossible struts. The clouded sky, not a building in sight except for the tops of those towers reaching.

The exterior of the tower that has replaced them reflects the sky.

The exhibition in the next room is about single-occupancy housing. The charts on the walls explain that only 1.5 per cent of New York City's rental housing stock is a studio or one-bedroom apartment ready for occupancy. This is inadequate for a modern population that wants to live alone. On display is an example of a new breed of apartment designed to meet the shortfall of single-occupancy housing. This apartment utilizes space by ensuring each piece of furniture performs a variety of functions. A woman is demonstrating all the places in the apartment where objects can be stored. The fold-out chairs can be hung on the wall when your guests have gone. The sofa folds down. A bed can be lowered from the wall. The footstool can be opened and a table taken out. The TV slides over to reveal a closet filled with regulated kitchenware. Edmund doesn't want to live alone. He crosses the room and looks out the window. Fifth Avenue has been closed to traffic. Outside, there is no space to move. It is teeming with people.

It is close to sunset. Soon it will be possible to see the black silhouette of the Eldorado Building on the other side of the park.

Edmund's phone vibrates.

An email from T.

Let's have dinner tonight, 8pm. Trattoria Spaghetto, Father Demo Square xx

Clockshower

(1973)

GORDON MATTA-CLARK

Gordon Matta-Clark climbs onto the stone ledge of the clock face and pulls himself up. He is hundreds of feet above New York. He reaches for the minute hand and steadies himself. On making contact with the minute hand a shower of water begins to fall. Gordon positions himself beneath the water, letting the water fall onto the rim of his black hat and then onto his coat and then his body then down his legs. He moves left and right to get the full flow of water directly onto his body. He moves the minute hand left and right so that the full flow of water drenches him. He reaches towards the clock face, and, from a fixed shelf there, he takes a toothbrush and a tube of toothpaste from a water glass then he squeezes the toothpaste onto the toothbrush and he brushes his teeth. After he has brushed his teeth he takes the water glass from the shelf and holds the water glass directly under the running water. He drinks water from the water glass then places the water glass back onto the shelf. He then takes a brush covered in shaving cream and he rubs the shaving cream over his cheeks and chin. He begins to shave. He starts with one cheek then the other then he moves onto his chin and then his upper lip.

He rinses his face in the water. He lies down under the clock face. He is covered head to toe in cream. Slowly, he sits up and moves the minute hand left and right to activate the water. He swings the minute hand back and forth and washes the cream away. He holds his leg up and washes the cream away. He sits up and directs the water onto his body, washing the cream away. He stands under the water. He takes an umbrella from the shelf and he holds it above his head so that he is protected from the falling water.

The camera pulls back, revealing New York City beneath him, the busy avenues and rivers of vehicles, the tiny people walking up and down the sidewalks, people crossing streets, the smoke and smog of industry, the distant view of ships in the harbour, water tanks and fire escapes, the grey sky above.

57

For the World's Fair in 1939 Robert Moses transformed Flushing Meadows in Queens from a landfill site into useable parkland with smooth lawns, recreational pavilions and landscaped walkways. He covered over trash with turf. He drained the marshes. He filled in the holes and landscaped the parkland, levelled out the avenues and boulevards, connected pathways, throughways and parking lots. But when he looked at the park left behind in 1940 he saw something unfinished, grass growing over unused ground, paths laid out but leading nowhere. All the parking lots were empty. The fair came and then it left. Nothing remained of it afterwards except the outline of a park.

The Chicago Fair in 1893 exhibited the technology behind the most recent phenomena – moving pictures, travelators, phosphorescent lamps. The World's Fair in Paris in 1889 exhibited a Wild West show, a human zoo and the Eiffel Tower. The fair in San Francisco in 1915 displayed exhibits about the Panama Canal, the aeroplane and the motor-car. In New York in 1939 the subject was 'The World of Tomorrow'. The theme of the 1964–65 New York World's Fair is 'Peace Through Understanding'. This time Robert Moses is in charge of it all. He organizes the building of a Walt Disney 'Small World' ride, a colour television studio, a Kodak Pavilion, the Westinghouse time capsule, a Transportation and Travel Pavilion. There is a 'Moon and Beyond' Cinerama. General Motors has an autoride into the future. The Amphitheatre puts on stage and water shows. There is a circus and a music hall with entertainers from Jones Beach. There's a Better Living Center, Pavilion of American Interiors, The House of Good Taste, a Little Old New York restaurant, a 7up International Sandwich Gardens, and a Coca-Cola's World of Refreshment. There is a Swiss Sky Ride, a Protestant Pavilion, a Mormon Pavilion, a Christian Science Pavilion and a Billy Graham Pavilion. The Vatican has a pavilion. The Federal Building contains a 'Challenge to Greatness' theatre and tributes to American heritage. The Carousel of Progress features life in the 1880s, 1920s, 1940s, and 1960s. There is a model of the plan for the World Trade Center. Chrysler exhibits an auto-production line. At the Illinois Pavilion there is an animatronic Abraham Lincoln and the Gettysburg Address.

Has there been much criticism, Commissioner? the reporter asks.

People like to criticize. Criticism doesn't build anything. Criticism is always negative. Always some fellow thinking he knows better than everybody else. Just look at what we've built here. You can't build something like this by listening to critics.

Will the fair be a success, Commissioner?

I believe it will be a success. All major structures and highways are complete. These were finished six weeks ahead of schedule. We had trouble getting the Belgian

Village started. It has a very complicated structure – a lot of work has gone into its historical accuracy – but we've done it. We've already sold fourteen hundred tickets. The critics can't argue with that. The thing about critics is that they don't build anything themselves. Now how can you trust a man who doesn't create anything?

Robert Moses is sitting with the reporter in the rear of a convertible as it travels slowly through a crowd of people down a pedestrianized street.

Moses says, Girls get confused over the numbers in memos. It's not their fault. They're not used to them. Some of these figures are very large. When we call this a billion-dollar fair, we mean a billion-dollar fair. We've widened the Grand Central Parkway without closing it to traffic. The Clearview Expressway has been completed. The Van Wyck Expressway has been widened. The Northern Boulevard has been given an elevated boulevard. The Whitestone Expressway has been extended. These changes will benefit New York long into the future. It is for the good of the city that we have made these changes.

Of course, there are always critics. I have a female friend, for example, who complained to me about the congestion surrounding the fair site. She said she was stuck in traffic for two hours outside the park. I said to her, 'Why did you go through at five o'clock on a Friday?' She said, 'I wanted to see what was going on.' There's nothing you can do about people like that.

A member of the public leans into the car and asks

Robert Moses for his autograph. Moses signs the paper and hands it back.

Are you satisfied with dedicating your life to building? asks the reporter.

Oh yes, I wouldn't do it otherwise, says Moses. I get appreciative letters from the public all the time. There's one man who has come to this fair thirty times. That experience is not uncommon. But there's a pathological desire in people to criticize. They say we've spent too much money on the fair and that the roads weren't needed. The press criticize because they're unhappy. Someone should look into their childhoods. All the fellow wants to know about are the states that didn't join the fair. The story is never about the states that did. Now, what do you do with a fellow like that? It makes no sense for New Yorkers to criticize New York. They are spreading the rumour that New York City is just a city of goons and thugs. People listen to gossip. Riots have kept people away from New York and that's the fault of the press. We've roamed these United States looking for pavilions and exhibits that will reflect the achievements of all men within industry, culture, the arts and entertainment. We confidently expect more than seventy million visitors to an unforgettable pageant.

Do you consider yourself a tough man, Commissioner?

Oh no, very mild.

The New York State Pavilion at the 1964–65 World's Fair will be a permanent new feature of Flushing Meadows–Corona Park. A circular area roofed with colourful Plexiglas tiles and two observation towers from where the public will view the fair.

As Moses and the reporter ride the Skystreak elevator to the top observation deck, the reporter asks, How have you risen above your critics?

I don't like to stay on their level, says Moses, laughing.

The reporter looks out over the fair. The expressways to the west of the park are jammed with vehicles, the automobiles as small as toys packed into traffic lanes. Crowds of people stream down the fair's many pathways.

There have been criticisms of your other projects, Commissioner. What do you say to critics like Jane Jacobs?

What do we care about the complaints? says Moses.

Some people say you've built this fair for yourself. Is this a monument to Robert Moses?

It isn't a monument to anyone.

They ride the carousel in the Belgian Village together. Moses is laughing as he tries to hang on.

I'm getting very friendly with the cashier, Moses says. By the third trip around, you've either made the conquest or you haven't!

Robert Moses is standing above the Panorama of the City of New York, a scale model of the city, two hundred and seventy-three blocks built by two hundred people over three years. Moses can see everything he ever built – the roadways, the housing, the beaches, the bridges. All the buildings in the model are made from wood and plaster but the bridges that Moses built are made from brass and built on a larger scale than the rest. The model shows the city as a system of neatly interconnected roadways, parkways and bridges. There are no people on the streets.

The reporter strolls around the model's perimeter walkway. The light effect changes from dawn to dusk. A lonely plastic aeroplane takes off and lands at La Guardia airport as the fake sun moves over. The model of the Unisphere, a great globe, is directly beneath him. Pavilions surround it. There are designated areas for refreshments and souvenir stalls. There is the General Motors Pavilion and an International Plaza. There is the Fountain of the Planets and a Belgian Village.

Robert Moses also built Jones Beach on Long Island. The reporter remembers visiting when he was young. He remembers the clear blue water of the diving pools and the changing rooms that had never been used. But he has been through this with his editor already. *Now don't get all gooey-eyed about this guy; just stick to the facts.*

Robert Moses is tall and broad, standing behind a lectern, looking casually over his audience. Behind him is the giant Unisphere positioned on its axis in the centre of a fountain.

This Fair is dedicated to man's achievement on a shrinking globe in an expanding universe, Moses says. The ambition of the fair is to provide good wholesome family fun, no cheap amusements or freak shows, no shabby games or bawdy entertainment. The central emblem of the fair is this steel Unisphere, a steel skeleton of the globe, hanging suspended over the central fountain, as tall as a twelve-storey building and made of corrosion-resistant steel. It is the largest replica of this planet ever constructed and will serve as a reminder of man's achievement long after the fair has gone. Bulldozers and builders, like poets, are incurable romantics at heart. This fair is the result of a pursuit of a dream. The dreamer is only as good as his dream.

The audience applauds. Moses turns to shake the hand of the representative from United States Steel Corporation. He accepts a large steel certificate.

A man leans over to the reporter and says, Do you know that this fair doesn't really exist? It doesn't have the backing of the Bureau of International Expositions. Moses charged exhibitors to erect their own pavilions but that's against the Bureau's rules. When they told him he wasn't allowed to charge he said to hell with you. So they've written him out of the history books. They won't endorse it. It'll hamper its chances. But Moses is a stubborn bastard.

Want to say that on the record?

Speak out against Robert Moses? He laughs. You've gotta be kidding.

58

You're not writing down what I am saying, says Walt.

Bucke looks down his notebook. The pages are blank.

59

When the body slows down, one thing goes and then another. It is like there is a list of final things for the body to do and once whoever it is who is in charge has given permission then that's when it starts, one thing followed by another. Everyone is watching Robert Mapplethorpe. They say this is how it should be for a photographer. As someone who has spent his whole life looking, in the end, it is him who must be watched. They say, Robert would want this, Robert would want that, but Robert can no longer speak.

He is dreaming of the Brooklyn docks. There is no grinding of ropes or hollers of foremen. No swing or snap of cargo and cranes. New York Bay is an inky swell of moonlight.

Then Midtown: cranes stand arrested in the night sky, great limbs, reaching for the morning. Scaffolding holds up newly constructed towers. The buildings are empty glass structures, an outer layer with nothing inside. They show how everything is formed – first the exterior is built and then it is filled. One day someone will look at the city from the other side of the glass and take a picture.

Welcome to the sixties.

Welcome to the last gasp.

Welcome to the hill brow.

Welcome to the shoulder stretch, the great dive, arms

outstretched, where Robert is standing in a muddy trench in Brooklyn during his military initiation, naked now, his feet sinking into mud, cold rain forming rivers of clear, pale skin down the length of his shins, and his whole body is aching. He is laughing.

Robert dies on the morning of March 9th 1989 at Deaconess Hospital in Boston. In his last moments he suffers a seizure, a terrible spasm, and then he is gone.

A necklace is lying on the bedside table. Edward has never seen Robert wear it. It is exotic, Persian. The plaques shimmer in the light. He looks at the necklace. He will take the necklace. He will give it to Patti. It was hers to begin with. He has heard the story many times.

60

Edmund showers and shaves. He arranges his hair. He sets out all of the bottles of toiletries neatly on the bathroom shelf. In the past he did not wash before going out. Now he wears aftershave and moisturizing cream. He wears hair cream and eyebrow gel. He wipes the steam from the mirror and looks at himself. He dresses in the bedroom, pulls on a pair of chinos and a loose-fitting shirt. He ties the laces of his shoes. He waits a moment to collect his thoughts. He reaches for the apartment door. He stops for a moment to look at his manuscript, the pages of which are loose and spread across the floor.

61

It happened for the first time when I was at work, says Walt. I had been feeling unwell all day and so I left work and walked home. When I got there I went straight to bed. I slept like I would never wake. I woke hours later. When I woke I could not move my arm or leg. I went back to sleep. When I woke again I could not move my body. I remained in bed. Time moved on but I could not. These attacks have persisted ever since. Though I am usually well, sometimes I find I cannot move. What do you think of this paralysis, Bucke? Is it a sign of something else, do you think? You are a medical man. Is there something I am doing wrong? I must finish my books. And there are so many letters to write. There's pleasure, Bucke, and love. What will happen when I am gone?

Bucke picks Walt's clothes up from the floor and folds them. He takes down the suitcase from the overhead compartment and lays the clothes neatly inside it. Bucke folds his own clothes and lays them in his trunk. Next he spreads his books evenly across the clothes to distribute the weight.

I recovered in my brother's house in Camden, says Walt. There is a railway track across the yard and all the trains in it are rusting. I lay very still in bed, surrounded by all the books and scraps of paper on which I had written many letters and poems. I realized this was the bed in which my mother died.

Bucke places his notebooks on top of his books and closes the lid of the trunk. He pushes the trunk and the suitcase towards the door where the porter will find them easily.

I arrived at my brother's house in time to see my mother die. She was no longer hungry. She could not eat. Her face was pale and sunken. She could no longer cough. Through the gap in the curtains I saw the rusting railway yard. I thought of other locations where I have known love.

Bucke separates the curtains and ties them.

I used to ride the streetcars in Washington. The ticket boy, Peter Doyle, had a pleasant face. He clipped my ticket many times on that first evening. He sat down beside me and placed his hand on my knee.

Bucke pulls on his overcoat and secures the buttons. He sits down before Walt.

As a printer I am aware of the shape and form of the poems on the page. It is not just the contents of a book that is important but also the parts that are left out. I print a page to see where the spaces are and then I know the poem I must write, I know its length and therefore its subject. I know how best to fill the space. When I look back through the book I can see the people described in it, the people who have inspired the poetry and the space in which they now reside. I see how they have now been reformed by the new context, in the pages of a book that forms a unit in itself, that is in itself whole. It starts with the recognition of blank space.

It starts with a beginning, how we see the things that could begin and then how they continue. It is in the spaces of the streets where we walk, long, wide avenues and the spaces in between them. It is in the organization of a map, laid out in a grid and the buildings that will one day be built within those spaces. I can see the borders of the island, how far we could go, and where we would have to stop. For isn't it true that this is life, that there is no end to this life, that we all are made from one another and will continue to form new time and new people and new ideas, and even when we are standing on the shoreline, stopped only by a body of water, we know we will continue like pages carried on a breeze. It is impossible for us to stop. I can see it all from above as if the city was a model on the ground. I see the blank spaces in the city and I can see how they might one day be filled. I see the pockets of neighbourhoods and their spreading outwards towards the shore. I see my beloved Brooklyn, and, further, the rest of Long Island. I see how each place is connected, how the rivers and ocean prevent them all from touching yet they are all connected under the water. It is all contained within me, this body. I am also a blank space, the space where things collect and form within my mind and within my body. I am the house and the book. I am the stanza and the sentence and the idea. The borders of these things are difficult to see. Ideas are not like islands for they cannot be fixed entirely on a map. I am finally putting it all into place. I have bought a plot of land, Bucke. I will be buried there. It does not matter where I am buried for when I am dead I will be dead in all places.

62

Edmund walks down Eighth Avenue, past KFC, Duane Reade, a Fashion College, three gyms, two dog parlours, West 23rd Street. People are mingling on the streets. The night is balmy and close. An orange glow cuts across the wide black avenue. Cars speed up then stop at lights.

Edmund hails a cab. The cab smells of cigar smoke. This makes him think of his father.

The cab drives through the orange fog. The streets are full. The stores are open. The restaurants are busy. All these things are familiar – the accents and the people speaking them, restaurants, delis, double-parking, but they have a different quality now, like Edmund is slowly losing his wider sense. He is extremely sensitive to vibration. There is a sense of the street rising to meet him. There is the movement of shadows, a tingle in his fingertips, in the end of his dick, an eyelash caught in the corner of his eye but when he feels for it he finds nothing there. The distant rumble of the subway, the thud of garbage being dumped in a basement, the scrape of a lock – the chain fence being secured across the Staten Island Ferry gangway, the slippery shift of feet upon metal, passengers eager to look out at the Statue of Liberty – oh, I thought she'd be taller, grander, still, this ride is free.

———

Edmund looks in the restaurant window. A family is crowding around a baby. A group is singing 'Happy Birthday' to a friend.

Yes?

A waiter beside him.

Edmund manages to say his own name.

Come with me, please, the waiter says. He is shown to a table and handed a menu. He surveys all the other tables around him. Edmund orders a carafe of wine. He has not drunk for many years.

Edmund looks up to see a man waving in the doorway. He is blond and athletic with a small, slender waist. He walks right over. Of course, he recognizes Edmund White.

Edmund, says T.

Edmund offers his hand. T shakes it, presses his fingers in.

You're early, T says.

I was in the neighbourhood. Would you like some wine? Edmund asks.

T sits down and takes the glass.

I can't believe you agreed to meet me, he says.

You said you were cute.

And am I?

Edmund smiles. This boy is very young. He is less than half Edmund's age. He is chewing a piece of bread and gulping his wine. Edmund feels a pang in his stomach as strong as any he knew in the past.

When the food arrives, Edmund is cautious not to eat too quickly. He doesn't want to be seen as having an appetite. He cuts his steak small and chews it slowly. He watches T take large mouthfuls. T is on his third glass of wine already. Their silence is disguised by the noises of others. Edmund wants to reach out his hand to touch T's. Years ago he would have done this. He would have reached across the table and taken his hand. He would have crawled under the table. But he doesn't do that now.

Robert Mapplethorpe's First Loft
(1999)

DEXTER DALWOOD

The painting depicts a dark room viewed through the segmentations of a chicken-wire screen. There is a black-sheeted bed, and the floor is black. The walls are black. At the end of the room is something red, a sofa or a table. Along one wall are two large windows. Here, sunlight hits the floor. Other sources of light include an overhead lamp and a mirror framed with lit bulbs. The glass mirror is bright white space. Nothing is being reflected here. There is a ceiling fan on the far side of the room. The room is empty. It is empty and dark except for the light coming from the mirror and the light coming in from the street. The artist has tried to replicate the feeling of the man through his absence. There is a sense in this painting that the man is out of the picture. There is a sense that this is as close as we can get. There are no people here. The painting is not realistic. The painting does not depict a real room. This room was never inhabited. It is the impression of a room. There is something of Robert Mapplethorpe in it, even though Robert Mapplethorpe has never been here. Perhaps it is more correct to say that we simply don't see him.

63

Patti handles the Persian necklace. She fingers the plaques and the clasp. She fits the necklace around her neck. The plaques are cold. They are heavy. Edward's fingers as he handed her the necklace looked for a moment like Robert's fingers. She unfastens the clasp. She places the necklace back in the drawer and switches off the light in her white room.

WORLD'S FAIR, FLUSHING MEADOWS –CORONA PARK, 1965

On the last day of the fair, two friends make their way to the General Motors Pavilion, where they have heard there is an exhibit about the future. The women get into the car and wait for the narration to begin.

It's almost a shame to know the future, one woman says. I don't think I want to know.

But the car is moving. They come to a diorama of the Moon with its large craters and grey, dusty surface. Animatronic men power lunar rovers to and from arrival pods. The Earth can be seen in the black sky.

The car climbs away from the Moon into Life Under the Ice where scientists are testing equipment in an ice-framed shelter. The narration explains they are testing weather monitors. One day they will be able to predict all future weather across the Earth.

Life Underwater follows. The woman begins to hold her breath. People are extracting minerals from the seabed. Vacationers peer through the glass walls of their hotel into the underwater wilderness.

Will we ever live in the jungle? The next diorama claims that we will. Trees are being knocked down with laser beams. Trees lie on the ground ready for processing. A machine is levelling the ground behind the fallen trees, creating a multilane highway behind it.

How awful, the woman says.

They are being pulled along the track to the land of the desert where crops have been planted and are thriving in specially irrigated fields. These crops do well in the sun, creating plenty of food for a rising population.

And then the City of Tomorrow. Monster skyscrapers and moving sidewalks, high-speed buses and mid-city airports. No one is walking any more, and everything is new.

Oh God, get me out of here, she says to her friend.

We can't just get off, her friend says.

She sits back down and waits for the ride to end.

When the ride is over, they hurry through the exit and into the fresh air. They fight their way through the crowd to the nearest patch of grass.

I'm exhausted. It's not even two o'clock.

We'll rest a moment, then we'll go on.

They watch the people walking by.

What do you want to do now?

See something else.

Something else?

I feel like a kid.

They follow the crowd to the time capsule, a sleek rocket-shaped container positioned on a stage.

They read in the programme the list of items that will be placed in the capsule: a Polaroid camera, an electric toothbrush, antibiotics, credit cards, a ballpoint pen, a bikini, a Beatles record.

Hmm, the friend says.

As the time capsule descends into the earth, the friend

notices a woman ripping up the flowers from the flower-beds beside her and shoving them into her handbag. Then she sees a man pull a poster from an advertising board. A woman runs out of a store holding a stack of chairs.

What's going on? she says to her friend.

Everyone wants a souvenir. It's the last day of the fair, she says.

64

Robert Mapplethorpe is cremated, segmented and organized – a vial for Patti, a box for his family.

Robert's memorial service is held in Queens. The people who come to it – the people who knew him from Manhattan – can't believe this is where he was born – post-war suburbia, wide, clean streets.

65

Edmund opens the book and dials the number. He requests a man who looks like T – tall, blond, athletic, young. He goes into the bathroom and washes his face. As the steam fogs the mirror he thinks about the steam engines of the elevated railway and the things he has seen. He thinks of Stephen Crane walking through New York at the turn of the twentieth century. He goes and stands at the living-room window. He looks down at the people on the street. There is a knock on the door.

Standing in the hallway is a young man of nineteen, maybe twenty. He must have been born in the nineteen-nineties. Edmund lays the money out on the table as the man undresses.

Where? says the man.

Here is OK.

The man takes Edmund's hand.

Feel this, the man says.

Edmund closes his eyes. This is the whole world: the city, skyscrapers and the hot street, this room, where love is happening.

66

The World's Fair closes sooner than expected. On its last day, the public raid it, rip the daffodils out from the flower-beds, rip the shelves out from the gift store, the cushions from cafeteria seats, the auditorium seats, ornaments, door handles, table tops. They are stripping the fair.

They swarm around Moses. Suddenly there is no room for him on the path. He takes a step sideways onto the grass. These ungrateful people. He built them a fair. He built them a city. He dedicated his life to them.

He remembers the burning effigy that the public carried through the Bronx after he tore their houses down. How he had laughed then. How funny it had seemed. But standing here, watching the looting, he is disturbed by the violence.

67

Bucke and Whitman are coming into the city.

Lights flicker in the windows. The silhouettes of the buildings, the blackness of the walls, the near black of the sky. Broadway, that great river, flowing upstream. Here are the people of the city – the men and women, the businessmen and those without jobs, the homeless and the traders of the city, the carts and the trolleys, the horses.

They sell so many Belgian waffles at the waffle stand that it is considered the most popular stand of the whole 1964–65 World's Fair. Coming here each day this summer, eating waffles every day for lunch as he takes a break from the games of chance, Robert Mapplethorpe is a beautiful young man. He stands in the Belgian Village beside the rotating carousel and eats the waffle from a cardboard holder, licking the sugar from his fingers, lighting a cigarette when he's done. The jackets and scarves of those on the carousel trail behind them. The smiles of the public are only moments and then they are gone. Robert flicks the butt away and wanders through the square towards the church. He stands a moment in the sun, thinking about which way to go. He continues into the crowd. So beautiful. I wonder what he will become.

NOTES

4   **Floral Park was a good place to come from** From the Robert Mapplethorpe Foundation website – http://www.mapplethorpe.org/biography/ – where the full quote is: 'Of his childhood he said, "I come from suburban America. It was a very safe environment and it was a good place to come from in that it was a good place to leave."'

23   **Once you sink that first stake** Robert A. Caro, *The Power Broker*, p. 218.

29   **Take us to the Chelsea** Patti Smith, *Just Kids*, p. 88. (Original dialogue reads, ' "Chelsea Hotel," I told the driver . . .')

30   **Because however cute the guy is** Patricia Morrisroe, *Mapplethorpe: A Biography*, p. 83. (Original dialogue reads, 'No matter how beautiful the guy was, I always asked for the money.')

56   **Edmund has called this book** Edmund White, *Hotel de Dream*, p. 223. (Exact quote is, 'This novel is my fantasia on real themes provided by history.')

67   ***You should meet me, I'm cute*** Edmund White, *My Lives*, p. 222.

80   ***This exhibition is about pleasure*** Sam Wagstaff, *A Book of Photographs From the Collection of Sam Wagstaff*, foreword. (Original text reads, 'This book is about pleasure, the pleasure of looking and the pleasure of seeing, like watching people dancing through an open window. They seem a little mad at first, until you realize they hear the song that you are watching.')

82   **He says that an obsession** Patricia Morrisroe,
Mapplethorpe: A Biography, p. 137. ('An obsession –
like any sort of love – is blinding.')

83   **I AM THE ARTIST** Ibid, p. 135. ('You're the collector,'
he reminded him. '*I'm* the artist.')

99   **You know, you should get a tattoo** Film, *Robert
Mapplethorpe with Peter Van de Klashorst*, April 1984.

124 **I always say you can draw any kind of picture** and
You can't make an omelette Robert A. Caro, *The Power
Broker*, p. 849. ('You can draw any kind of picture you
like on a clean slate and indulge your every whim in
the wilderness in laying out a New Delhi, Canberra or
Brasilia, but when you operate in an overbuilt
metropolis, you have to hack your way with a meat ax.')

125 **You mean, besides a waste of time?** Film, *Mr
Mackridge Interviews Mr Moses*, 1963 (New York Public
Library, New York World's Fair 1964–65 Corporation
Records. Original dialogue: "What do you call
relaxation?" "You mean do I say it's a waste of time?").

134 **There are a number of things I must insist on** Based
on Hard Times Tour, Tenement Museum, New York
City.

141 *What was once a run-down* PBS Documentary, *The
World That Moses Built*, 1989.

142 *What do I believe?* CBS documentary, *The Man Who
Built New York*, 1963.

214 **I think the urn is Persian** and **They look more like
pieces of shell** Film, Steven Sebring, *Dream of Life*,
2008.

231 *What message do people have* Real speech from film
of Whitney Opening, 1988, held at the Getty Research
Institute.

238 **Has there been much criticism, Commissioner?**

Dialogue from documentary, *New York New York: The Fair Face of Robert Moses*, 1964 (NYPL World's Fair 1964–65 archives).

239 **Girls get confused over the numbers** Sound recording, *Press Conference on Arterials*, 1963 (NYPL World's Fair 1964–65 archives).

240 **Are you satisfied with dedicating your life to building?** Dialogue from documentary, *New York New York: The Fair Face of Robert Moses*, 1964 (NYPL World's Fair 1964–65 archives).

241 **How have you risen above your critics?** Ibid.

241 **I'm getting very friendly with the cashier** Ibid.

242 **This Fair is dedicated to man's achievement** Sound recording, *Unisphere Presentation*, 1964 (NYPL World's Fair 1964–65 archives).

SOURCES

BOOKS

ROBERT MAPPLETHORPE

Robert Mapplethorpe: A Biography, Macmillan, London, 1995
    – Patricia Morrisroe
Just Kids, Bloomsbury, London, 2010 – Patti Smith
Mapplethorpe: Assault With a Deadly Camera, Hastings House,
    Mamaroneck, NY, 1994 – Jack Fritscher
The Basketball Diaries, Penguin, London, 1995 – Jim Carroll
Forced Entries, Penguin, London, 1987 – Jim Carroll

EDMUND WHITE

City Boy, Bloomsbury, London, 2009 – Edmund White
My Lives, Bloomsbury, London, 2005 – EW
A Boy's Own Story, Picador, London, 1994 – EW
Forgetting Elena, and Nocturnes for the King of Naples, Pan
    Books, London, 1984 – EW
The Farewell Symphony, Vintage, London, 1998 – EW
Hotel de Dream, Bloomsbury, London, 2007 – EW
The Burning Library, Chatto & Windus, London, 1994 – EW
The New Joy of Gay Sex, GMP Publishers, London, 1993 –
    EW, Charles Silverstein and Felice Picano

ROBERT MOSES

The Power Broker: Robert Moses and the Fall of New York,
    Knopf, New York, 1974 – Robert A. Caro

Robert Moses and the Modern City: The Transformation of New York, W. W. Norton, New York, 2008 – Hilary Ballon and Kenneth T. Jackson

The Death and Life of Great American Cities, Vintage, London, 1993 – Jane Jacobs

Theory and Practice in Politics, Godkin Lectures, Cambridge, Mass., 1940 – Robert Moses

Working For the People: Promise and Performance in Public Service, Harper, 1956 – Robert Moses

WALT WHITMAN

Leaves of Grass, Library of America, 2011 – Walt Whitman

Walt Whitman, David McKay, Philadelphia, 1883 (facsimile edition by BiblioLife) – Richard Maurice Bucke

Man's Moral Nature: An Essay, Trübner, London, 1879 – RMB

Cosmic Consciousness, Dover Publications, Mineola, New York, 2009 (originally published by E. P. Dutton, Inc., New York, 1929) – RMB

Walt Whitman: A Song of Himself, University of California Press, 1999 – Jerome Loving

Specimen Days In America, The Folio Society, London, 1979 – Walt Whitman

The Portable Whitman, Penguin, 1977 – ed. Mark Van Doren

ART BOOKS

Polaroids: Mapplethorpe, Prestel, Munich, 2007 – Sylvia Wolf

Altars, Cape, London, 1995 – Robert Mapplethorpe and Edmund White

Pistils, Jonathan Cape, London, 1996 – Robert Mapplethorpe

Flowers, Schirmer/Mosel, Munich, 2014 – Robert Mapplethorpe and Patti Smith

Lady, Lisa Lyon, Blond & Briggs, London, 1983 – Robert Mapplethorpe and Bruce Chatwin

Robert Mapplethorpe, Whitney Museum of American Art in
       ass. with New York Graphic Society Books, New York,
       1988 – Richard Marshall, Ingrid Sischy, Richard
       Howard

Some Women, Secker & Warburg, London, 1989 – Robert
       Mapplethorpe

Certain People: A Book of Portraits, Twelve Trees Press,
       Pasadena, CA, 1985 – Robert Mapplethorpe

Robert Mapplethorpe, National Galleries of Scotland,
       Edinburgh, 2006 – Robert Mapplethorpe

Robert Mapplethorpe and the Classical Tradition, Guggenheim
       Museum, New York, 2004 – Germano Celant and
       Arkady Ippolitov

A Book of Photographs From the Collection of Sam Wagstaff,
       Gray Press, Rochester, New York, 1978 – Sam Wagstaff

The Ballad of Sexual Dependency, Aperture, New York, 2012
       – Nan Goldin

I'll Be Your Mirror, Whitney Museum of American Art & Scalo,
       New York, 1996 – Nan Goldin

*Mixed Use Manhattan: Photography and Related Practices,
       1970s to the present*, MIT Press, London, 2010 –
       Douglas Crimp, Lynne Cooke, Kristin Poor

Exposed: Voyeurism, Surveillance and the Camera, Tate,
       London, 2010 – Sandra S. Philips

On the Museum's Ruins, MIT Press, London, 1993 – Douglas
       Crimp and Louise Lawler

Evictions: Art and Spatial Politics, MIT Press, London, 1996 –
       Rosalyn Deutsche

*Playing With the Edge: The Photographic Achievement of Robert
       Mapplethorpe*, University of California Press, London,
       1996 – Arthur Danto

Site-Specific Art: Performance, Place and Documentation,
       Routledge, London, 2000 – Nick Kaye

Soho: The Artist in the City, University of Chicago Press,
London, 1981 – Charles R. Simpson

The Downtown Book: The New York Art Scene 1974–1984,
Princeton University Press, Princeton, 2006 – various

Pornography or Art?, Words and Pictures, Harrow, 1971 – Poul
Gerhard

*Reading American Photographs: Images as History, Mathew
Brady to Walker Evans*, Hill and Wang, New York, 1989
– Alan Trachtenberg

*Inside the Studio: Two Decades of Talks with Artists in New
York*, Independent Curators International, New York,
2004 – Judith Olch Richards

BACKGROUND READING

How the Other Half Lives, Dover Publications, London, 1971
– Jacob Riis

*Branding New York: How a City in Crisis Was Sold to the
World*, Routledge, London, 2008 – Miriam Greenberg

Naked City: The Death and Life of Authentic Urban Places,
Oxford University Press, Oxford, 2010 – Sharon Zukin

Between Ocean and City, Columbia University Press, New
York, 2003 – Lawrence and Carol Kaplan

*City of Eros: NYC, Prostitution and the Commercialisation of
Sex, 1790–1920*, W. W. Norton, London, 1994 –
Timothy J. Gilfoyle

*Fragmented Urban Images: The American City in Modern
Fiction from Stephen Crane to Thomas Pynchon*, P. Lang,
New York, 1991 – Gerd Hurm

Imperial City: The Rise and Rise of New York, Ulverscroft, 1989
– Geoffrey Moorhouse

*Inventing Times Square: Commerce and Culture at the
Crossroads of the World*, Russell Sage Foundation, New
York, 1991 – William R. Taylor

Leadership, Time Warner, London, 2003 – Rudolph Giuliani

Pornography Without Prejudice: A Reply to Objectors, Abelard-Schuman, London, 1972 – Geoff L. Simons

Prurient Interests: Gender, Democracy and Obscenity in New York City, 1909–1945, Columbia University Press, New York, 2000 – Andrea Friedman

Public Sex/Gay Space, Columbia University Press, Chichester, New York, 1999 – William Leap

Slumming: Sexual and Racial Encounters in American Nightlife 1885–1940, University of Chicago Press, Chicago, 2009 – Chad Heap

Take Back the Night: Women on Pornography, Bantam, London, 1982 – ed. Laura Lederer

The Assassination of New York, Verso, London, 1993 – Robert Fitch

The Disappearance of Objects: New York and the Rise of the Postmodern City, Yale University Press, London, 2009 – Joshua Shannon

The Skyscraper, Allen Lane, London, 1982 – Paul Goldberger

The Times Square Story, W.W. Norton, London, 1998 – Geoffrey O'Brien

Times Square Red Times Square Blue, New York University Press, London, 1999 – Samuel R. Delany

Times Square Roulette: Remaking the City Icon, MIT Press, London, 2001 – Lynne B. Sagalyn

Brooklyn Bridge: Fact and Symbol, University of Chicago Press, Chicago, 1979 – Alan Trachtenberg

On Photography, Penguin, London, 1979 – Susan Sontag

Camera Lucida: Reflections on Photography, Flamingo, London, 1984 – Roland Barthes

The Denial of Death, Free Press, London, 1973 – Ernest Becker

Illness as Metaphor and AIDS *and its Metaphors*, Penguin, London, 2002 – Susan Sontag

Gotham: A History of New York City to 1898, Oxford University Press, Oxford, 2000 – Edwin Burrows

The City That Never Was, Viking, London, 1988 – Rebecca Shanor

New York 1930 (Rizzoli, New York 1987) */1960* (Taschen, Koln, 1997) */2000* (Monacelli Press, New York, 2006) – Robert A. M. Stern

Twenty Minutes in Manhattan, Reaktion Books, London, 2009 – Michael Sorkin

After the World Trade Center: Rethinking New York City, Routledge, London, 2002 – Michael Sorkin and Sharon Zukin

The New York Approach: Robert Moses, Urban Liberals and the Redevelopment of the Inner City, Ohio State University Press, 1993 – Joel Schwartz

Urban Theory and Urban Experience: Encountering the City, Routledge, London, 2004 – Simon Parker

The Urban Lifeworld: Formation, Perception and Representation, Routledge, London, 2002 – Peter Madsen and Richard Plunz

Starting From Zero: Reconstructing Downtown New York, Routledge, London, 2003 – Michael Sorkin

The New Deal and the Unemployed: The View from New York City, Bucknell University Press, 1979 – Barbara Blumberg

This Wild Darkness: The Story of My Death, Fourth Estate, London, 1996 – Harold Brodkey

AIDS, *Cultural Analysis/Cultural Activism*, MIT Press, London, 1988 – Douglas Crimp

FILMS

Video of Spanish television documentary on Robert
 Mapplethorpe, 1980s, box 196, Robert Mapplethorpe
 Papers, J. Paul Getty Trust, Getty Research Institute,
 Los Angeles

Whitney Opening with Robert Mapplethorpe, 1988, Robert
 Mapplethorpe Papers, J. Paul Getty Trust, Getty
 Research Institute, Los Angeles

Robert Mapplethorpe with Peter Van de Klashorst, 1984, box
 196, Robert Mapplethorpe Papers, J. Paul Getty Trust,
 Getty Research Institute, Los Angeles

*Black, White + Gray: A Portrait of Sam Wagstaff and Robert
 Mapplethorpe* by James Crump, 2007

Arena, by Nigel Finch, 1988, box 196, Robert Mapplethorpe
 Papers, J. Paul Getty Trust, Getty Research Institute,
 Los Angeles

Lady, by Robert Mapplethorpe, 1984, box 197, Robert
 Mapplethorpe Papers, J. Paul Getty Trust, Getty
 Research Institute, Los Angeles

Dream of Life, by Steven Sebring, 2008

Mr Mackridge Interviews Mr Moses, 1963, 01144, New York
 World's Fair 1964–65 Corporation Records, New York
 Public Library, New York City

The Man Who Built New York, 1963, 00642, New York World's
 Fair 1964–65 Corporation Records, New York Public
 Library, New York City

New York New York: The Fair Face of Robert Moses, 00668,
 New York World's Fair 1964–65 Corporation Records,
 New York Public Library, New York City

Cruising directed by William Friedkin, 1980

Sound Recordings

Unisphere Presentation, 1964, 01175, New York World's Fair
    1964–65 Corporation Records, New York Public Library,
    New York City
Press Conference on Arterials, 1963, 01123, New York World's
    Fair 1964–65 Corporation Records, New York Public
    Library, New York City
The Coral Sea by Patti Smith, 2008
Patti Smith: The Classic Interview, 2009

Online Sources

1853 NYC World's Fair exhibition programme
'Off the Shelf', article in the *New Yorker*, 10 October 2011
'The Other Mapplethorpe' article in the *Observer*, 2007
ZIP Magazine Interview with Edward Mapplethorpe (YouTube)
'The Eye of Sam Wagstaff' by Bruce Hainley, *Artforum*, April
    1997
'American Experience: The World That Moses Built', PBS
    documentary (You Tube)
1964/65 World's Fair Futurama Ride film (YouTube)
The Robert Mapplethorpe Foundation

Interviews conducted

Patricia Morrisroe, author, biographer of Robert Mapplethorpe
Sarah Forbes, Curator, Museum of Sex, New York City
Yona Backer, Founder of Third Streaming, Agent of The Alvin
    Baltrop Trust, New York City

Third Streaming, home of Alvin Baltrop estate, New York City
Robert Moses Papers, New York World's Fair 1964–65
      Corporation Records, Walt Whitman Papers, New York
      Public Library, New York City
Robert Mapplethorpe Papers, Sam Wagstaff Papers, J. Paul
      Getty Trust, Getty Research Institute, Los Angeles
National Library of Scotland, Edinburgh
Robert Mapplethorpe Collection, National Galleries of
      Scotland, Edinburgh
'Pioneers of the Downtown Scene, New York 1970s', Barbican,
      London, 2011
'Robert Mapplethorpe: Nightwork', Alison Jacques Gallery,
      London, 2011
'Ballad of Sexual Dependency', Whitney Museum, New York
      City, 2013
'Hard Times' Tour, Tenement Museum, New York City, 2008
      & 2013
High Line Park, New York City, 2013
Museum of the City of New York, New York City, 2013
Museum of Sex, New York City, 2013
Times Square Visitor Center, New York City, 2013

Acknowledgements

I wouldn't have been able to write this book without the love and support of my husband, best friend and writing partner, Ben Smart, with whom I can accomplish anything.

Thank you to everyone at Picador and Pan Macmillan for welcoming me so warmly. Thank you to Paul Baggaley and Sophie Jonathan for their passionate belief, intelligent editing, and for making this a better book. Thank you also to Nicholas Blake for his attention to detail, to Lucie Cuthbertson-Twiggs for her ideas, and to Ami Smithson for her exquisite artwork.

Thank you to Sophie Lambert for her inexhaustible faith, determination, and friendship, and to the foreign rights team at Conville & Walsh for their hard work.

Thank you to Mum and Dad for their encouragement, support and belief, and for never suggesting I 'get a proper job'.

Thank you to Elsie Jenkins – reader, writer, thinker – she showed me the ropes.

Thank you to Kirsty, Rhiannon, Karl, Jude, Eda, Gary, Patricia, Alan, Liz, Rachel, David, Rosie and Jacca for their unconditional love, which has sustained me.

To my fellow lister and bosom friend, Kirsten Irving – thank you for championing me on a weekly basis, for pointing out all the things I have done, and for encouraging me to complete all the things still left to do.

Thank you to all who read the book in its early stages: Lauren Frankel, Nick DeSpain, Joe Dunthorne, Tom Benn, Mischa Pearlman and Tommy Karshan. Thank you to Phil Cooper for his beautiful designs and to Armando Celayo for his advice.

To the best friends a woman could have: Daisy Bourne, Beth Settle, Alex Ivey and Shubhangi Swarup – thank you for the pep talks, and for making me laugh.

Thank you to Natasha Soobramanien and Luke Williams for giving me the confidence to write this to begin with.

Thank you to the best teachers I've ever had, Andrew Cowan and Ian Hinde, who taught me the art of self-belief.

Thank you to Jean McNeil and Ali Smith for making me realize what I could do, for their support and encouragement, and for their incredible books, which have inspired me.

Thank you to Val Taylor, Michèle Roberts, Patricia Duncker, David Flusfeder, and Bernardine Evaristo for steering me onto the right road, and thank you to Cathi Unsworth for ensuring I stay on it.

I'd like to thank the following institutions for allowing me to access their archives and collections during my research for this book: thank you to the National Galleries of Scotland; the National Library of Scotland; the Edinburgh Public Library; the New York Public Library; the Getty Research Institute; the Robert Mapplethorpe Foundation; New York's Museum of Sex; and Third Streaming.

Thank you to Patricia Morrisroe, Sarah Forbes, Yona Backer and Isabel Vincent for their valuable time.

Thank you to Will Boast and Johnny Levin for providing me with a home in America.

I am also indebted to the many biographers, historians, art critics and urban commentators (listed on pages 267–75) whose work contributed to my research, and without whom this book couldn't have been written.

I have been lucky enough to have had feedback, professional advice and letters of support from many individuals and organizations. Thank you to Martin Pick, Chris Gribble, Jon Cook, George Szirtes, Kevin Conroy-Scott, Briony Bax, everyone at *Ambit*, the Writers Centre Norwich, and the board of the Charles Pick Fellowship.

Thank you to the University of East Anglia, which has nurtured my writing over many years.

I am also grateful to Arts Council England for their generous grant.

Thank you to those whose work has helped me to indulge my obsession with New York City during the writing of this book: Lou Reed, Woody Allen, and Tom Meyers and Greg Young from the Bowery Boys (www.boweryboyshistory.com).

Thank you to Todd Haynes, whose film, *I'm Not There*, provided the light bulb moment.

Thank you to Don DeLillo, whose books have inspired me and made me a better writer.

Thank you to the artists whose work lit a fire in my belly: Patti Smith, Laurie Anderson, Nan Goldin, Gordon Matta-Clark, Richard Serra, Alvin Baltrop, Jacob Riis, Steven Sebring, Edward Mapplethorpe, Edward J. Steichen, David Wojnarowicz, and Dexter Dalwood.

And thank you to the subjects at the heart of it all: to New York City, which opened my eyes, and to Robert Mapplethorpe, Edmund White, Robert Moses and Walt Whitman, who showed me which way to look.